DATE DUE

27 Magic Words

27
Magic Words

Sharelle Byars Moranville

Saxton B. Little Free Library
310 Route 87
Columbia, CT 06237
10/16

HOLIDAY HOUSE / NEW YORK

★

Copyright © 2016 by Sharelle Byars Moranville
All Rights Reserved
HOLIDAY HOUSE is registered in the U.S. Patent and Trademark Office.
Printed and bound in June 2016 at Maple Press, York, PA, USA
First Edition
1 3 5 7 9 10 8 6 4 2
www.holidayhouse.com

Library of Congress Cataloging-in-Publication Data
Names: Moranville, Sharelle Byars, author.
Title: 27 magic words / Sharelle Byars Moranville.
Other titles: Twenty-seven magic words
Description: First edition. | New York : Holiday House, [2016] | Summary:
Although Kobi's parents sailed into a storm five years ago, she believes
they are alive, and when she is sent from her grandmother's luxurious
Paris apartment to live with an uncle in Iowa, Kobi tells lies that soon
catch up with her.
Identifiers: LCCN 2015049142 | ISBN 9780823436576 (hardcover)
Subjects: | CYAC: Truth—Fiction. | Self-perception—Fiction. |
Grief—Fiction.
Classification: LCC PZ7.M78825 Aah 2016 | DDC [Fic]—dc23 LC record
available at https://lccn.loc.gov/2015049142

Saxton B. Little Free Library

To my husband, Barry

Contents

· · · · · · · · · · · · · · · · ·

RAZZMATAZZ

ONE
(San Francisco)

*O*NE September morning when Kobi was new to kindergarten, her dad, the Great Alighieri, came to their classroom and did magic. He pulled Dante out of a flowerpot. He made daisies grow from a girl's head. And he drew miles and miles of colorful silk scarves out of a tiny gold box. At the end, when he called Kobi up to take a bow with him, she had never felt more important.

And then he dropped her and Dante off at home and went to his office.

Their house had never seemed so dull. The soup bowls were a boring brown, the table was a boring brown, the floor was a boring brown.

"Why don't *you* do magic?" she said to her mother as

they ate their boring lunch of ramen noodles. "Like the Great Alighieri."

"Pfh!" her mother said. "He does razzmatazz. I do serious magic."

Kobi stared. Her mother never did anything exciting.

"Every day, I make people fall in love." Her mother snapped her fingers the way the Great Alighieri did when a Ping-Pong ball popped out of an ear. "I make annoying people wander into poison ivy." She flicked her finger as if it were a wand.

Kobi looked around the room, the hair rising on her arms. "Where?"

Her mother took a book off the shelf. "They live in here."

Kobi held the book in her lap and looked at her mother's picture on the back. She opened it. The words were long and close together. There were no pictures.

"Does Brook know about your magic?" Kobi asked.

Her mother shook her head. "Let's keep it our secret."

The younger daughter of the Great Alighieri knew something the older daughter didn't. Kobi smiled.

They sat with the window open, listening to the trolley clatter down the hill.

"You have to let me work now," Kobi's mom said after a while. She kissed Kobi and winked at her. "Remember. Serious magic. Our secret." She rolled her chair to her desk and opened her laptop.

Kobi found her pillow, as she did every afternoon. She crawled into the hideaway behind her mother's desk, the hideaway that the Great Alighieri had made when Brook went off to kindergarten last year. No one but he could find her when she was in the secret pocket lined with pink velvet.

Kobi listened to her mother's fingers flying across the keyboard. Her mother's toes were not very far from Kobi's face. They were wiggling as if something exciting were happening somewhere.

"Give me one of your magic words," Kobi said.

The toes stopped moving. "Please?"

"Please," Kobi said.

Her mother's hand, holding a yellow Post-it note, appeared in front of Kobi's face. Kobi pulled the Post-it off her mother's finger and looked at it. "I can't read long words."

Her mother cleared her throat, which meant Kobi should try. There were a lot of zs. Kobi made a buzzing noise.

Her mother gave her a hint. "Razz?"

"Razzmatazz!"

The house began to tremble, the windows began to rattle, and the glasses in the china cupboard began to jingle. Kobi gripped the bit of paper, wondering if she was strong enough to hold such magic. She wanted to give it back, but she also wanted to keep it.

She stuck the word on her shirt right over her heart. "Another!" she cried, wondering if her mother would do such a bold thing. "Please."

A Post-it appeared in front of her nose. "What does it say?" Kobi asked.

"*Squelch,*" her mother said.

"Squelch?" Kobi repeated. It made her laugh.

"What?" her mom asked.

"It feels funny in my mouth."

"You're silly," her mother said. But she said "*Squelch*" and giggled.

"Squelch," Kobi said.

Gradually the tinkle of the glasses in the china cupboard faded away. The words were very powerful.

"May I have another?"

She took it off her mother's finger. "Phyllo bundle," her mother said. "Now let me work, please. It's time for your nap."

Kobi looked at the words *Phyllo bundle* as she lay back on her pillow, beginning to get cozy. She tucked the Post-its under her pillow and rolled up in her blanket.

★

In the quiet afternoons, her mother gave her more words. Most were written on yellow Post-its, some were written on orange, and a few were written on neon green. Her mother gave Kobi twenty-seven magic words before she and the Great Alighieri disappeared.

AVANTI!

TWO
(Paris, almost five years later)

*T*HE breeze ruffled Kobi's growing-out bangs. Grandmamma said cups should have saucers and girls should have bangs, but Kobi planned to grow her hair to all one length like her mother's.

From the balcony, the sky was a soft blue. Over the old Parisian apartment buildings with their copper roofs, enormous clouds billowed. They made Kobi think of the sails on their parents' boat.

When the doorbell sounded, she sighed and went in. The word to ward off annoying people was *fiddlesticks*. It made the concierge stop talking Grandmamma's ear off when Grandmamma's feet were tired, for example. But magic words didn't work when they were used selfishly. So Kobi didn't bother trying, because Brook *loved* Mademoiselle—as did Grandmamma and Madame Louise.

Brook stopped scribbling in her diary and swung her legs over the edge of the tall bed, which required a ladder for ladylike egress.

"Let's hide from Mademoiselle," Kobi suggested.

"That might hurt her feelings," Brook said.

Mademoiselle LeBlanc came with worksheets and lesson plans every Monday, Wednesday, and Thursday. Kobi preferred the other two days of the week. Sometimes they had educational outings with other kids on those days. Sometimes they hung out with Grandmamma or Madame Louise, their housekeeper. This morning, Grandmamma was out somewhere with her friend Mr. Gyver.

✹

The voices of Mademoiselle and Madame Louise grew soft as the women drifted to the back of the apartment. Maybe they would gossip over tea and forget about lessons.

Kobi glanced into the foggy antique mirror that stood in the corner of their bedroom. Would her parents even recognize her when they got home? Her dad wouldn't be able to pull her onto his lap and call her his little bunny anymore. Would he call her his big rabbit?

"Do you suppose Daddy took Dante with him on the trip?" she asked Brook. "And forgot to tell us?"

When they were little, the sweet white rabbit had let Kobi and Brook dress him in doll clothes and wrap him in napkins. He had his own chair at the table in the kitchen of their San Francisco house. He liked to sleep on their mother's bare feet. He belonged to their dad, the Great Alighieri.

"You shouldn't still be thinking about Dante," Brook said, her lips set.

"A person can't help their thoughts. They pop up."

After their parents had left on their sailing trip, Kobi and Brook had looked everywhere for Dante. Grandmamma helped them search the big blue house that overlooked the bay. Sometimes Dante hid in crannies.

But the weeks passed and they never saw Dante again. When Grandmamma closed the San Francisco house so they could move to Paris, Kobi taped a picture of him on the kitchen cupboard along with a note explaining what he liked to eat and where she could be reached. She whispered, *"Temporarily,"* as she kissed his picture. That magic word helped things get better for unfortunate people, and surely it would work for bunnies, too.

In front of the mirror, Brook smoothed her bangs and tidied the ribbon that held her hair back. Recently she had started rubbing lotion on her hands and using a second mirror to see her back.

"I wish we could have an adventure," Kobi said. Outside, there would be things to do on the boulevard. Shop-windows to peer into, dogs on leashes to pet, ducks to feed in the park.

"Mademoiselle doesn't like adventures," Brook said.

Mademoiselle liked multiple-choice questions, tidy writing, correct French, aspirational reading, and little gold stars. Grandmamma said often how grateful she was for Mademoiselle. Grandmamma said someday, someday *way in the future*, Kobi and Brook would be going back to the U.S. and they would be able to segue into the American school system.

Brook had carried the word *segue* as proudly as the concierge's cat with a water bug. She dropped it at the feet of Mademoiselle. Mademoiselle buttered Brook on both sides with praise. Kobi had been tempted to tell them about *her* words, the twenty-seven that she had brought to Paris in her footlocker, the magic words, some of which were much finer than *segue*. But she didn't because her mother had said they were secret.

Kobi flung herself into an easy chair and swiveled to stare at the sky. "I'll be *so* glad when they're home."

The bathroom door closed quietly. Kobi heard water running.

"Brook?" she said, her hand on the doorknob. After a bit, she tapped on the door. "May I come in?"

The water went off. Brook opened the door, drying her hands on the little linen towel with an *M* for Mallory, Grandmamma's last name, embroidered in one corner.

"Let's go find Mademoiselle," Kobi said.

Brook nodded, but before they were ten steps away from the bathroom, she turned back. "I have to check . . ."

Kobi knew Brook was making sure the faucet was turned off.

The fourth time, they got partway down the hall before Brook went back. It was Kobi's fault, talking about Dante and their parents.

"There you are!" Mademoiselle called. "Time for lessons."

"Wait," Brook said, turning around. "I have to . . ."

Mademoiselle raised her eyebrows at Kobi.

Kobi nodded.

When Brook returned from the bathroom, Mademoiselle put her arms around Brook's shoulders and said, "I have a basket of cherries from my morning walk. Perhaps we should do something interesting with them."

Brook's face brightened. "We could follow a recipe."

"I'm sure Madame Louise has a recipe for cherry something or other."

"If you follow the recipe exactly," Brook told Kobi, as if Kobi hadn't heard it a thousand times, "everything turns out right at the end."

In the kitchen, the sun threw squares of light over the counters. Mademoiselle uncovered the small basket of cherries.

"The cherries aren't very big," Brook said.

"They're wild. I foraged them along the alley," Mademoiselle said. "I was very lucky to get them before the birds did."

Since there weren't very many, and they weren't very big,

Madame Louise got out little white ramekins and suggested they make mini clafoutis.

Kobi had no idea that pitting the tiny, sour cherries would be so interesting. Her hands ended up as stained as if she'd butchered a pig, not that she would do such a thing. She loved to pet Mr. Gyver's pigs when they went to his farm. Mr. Gyver was from the U.S. like Kobi, Brook, and Grandmamma, but he was an expert in world food supplies and had lived in France for years. Kobi sniffed her red fingers. They smelled like almonds, which Mademoiselle said was from the cherry pits.

Once the mini clafoutis were in the oven and they were washing dishes, Mademoiselle set a math problem involving the grams of pitted cherries, the volume of each ramekin, and some fraction or other. Kobi could hear Brook's brain clicking happily away. She herself did not find math interesting.

She slipped into the pantry and out the window onto the fire escape, which Grandmamma said they weren't to do. But Kobi loved spying on the alley. Today, after several minutes, nothing was happening except two squirrels chasing each other. And the cherry juice on her hands was attracting bees.

Someone grabbed her arm. "Kobi Alighieri!"

Grandmamma hauled her over the windowsill into the pantry. "What if you fell? You would splat on the bricks in the alley. . . ." She hugged Kobi close, enveloping her. "Oh my. I'm too old for this." Grandmamma sat on the windowsill, fanning her face with her hand. She pulled Kobi onto her lap though Kobi was too big. "What would I do if something happened to you?"

Grandmamma was truly scared, and Kobi said sorry. She looked at her feet because she couldn't bear to look at Grandmamma's face.

Grandmamma sighed, released Kobi's hands, and said, "*Do not* go out this window again."

Later, after the warm clafoutis were eaten, Kobi and Brook went to the schoolroom to take turns reading from the *Le Petit Nicolas* series. Kobi read in French, and Brook translated into English, and then they switched. Mademoiselle used the story to drill them in sentence structure and French idioms.

After lunch, Mademoiselle placed a yellow gentian in a vase on the drawing table. She pronounced it a miracle, since it was a Pyrenees wildflower and had no business growing in her alley, where she had found it. She suggested the girls make a botanical drawing of the plant.

Since it was only a suggestion, Kobi didn't take it. Botanical drawings were stiff and boring. Kobi wanted to paint something that Grandmamma would pronounce *interesting!*

One of Kobi's creations that Grandmamma found *interesting* hung on the dining room wall beside the Louis XV mirror. It looked important there. Her parents would admire it when they came to get her and Brook. Kobi would pretend at first not to care much that they were back or liked her painting. It would be what they deserved for going off and leaving them in the first place.

Brook and Mademoiselle were slicing the poor gentian open from top to bottom and asked Kobi to come look.

"Eew," Kobi said. She had seen flower private parts before.

The best use of flowers was their names. *Honeysuckle, trillium,* and *veronica* were great for finding things like Mr. Gyver's umbrella, Grandmamma's reading glasses, and Madame Louise's shopping list.

Brook called Grandmamma to come and look at the gentian. Grandmamma said she had liked it better in the vase.

"What should I paint?" Kobi asked Grandmamma.

Grandmamma stood behind Kobi and looked at the canvas on the easel. Kobi leaned back, feeling Grandmamma's softness and breathing in her *Freesia* perfume. That was one of the words her mother had given her. Grandmamma began to massage Kobi's scalp. If Kobi had been a cat, she would have arched her back and twined between Grandmamma's ankles, purring. *Freesia* was a purring word.

"I have a million things to do," Grandmamma said finally, kissing Kobi's head. "I'll be in my study."

"But what shall I paint?"

"Paint a story about something important."

Kobi liked stories. And Grandmamma was important. She had traveled from Paris to San Francisco to stay with them while their parents went on their sailing trip. She had helped Brook and Kobi make madeleine cakes and set up a lemonade stand after Brook got home from school. She had showed them how to weave a cat's cradle with their fingers and purple yarn. She had taught them to eat fig preserves. She hugged and kissed them a trillion times.

For the first three weeks their parents were gone, they called every night at bedtime. Their dad had purchased an extra copy of *Mr. Popper's Penguins* to take on the trip, and he read to them while Brook and Kobi followed along in their book.

Then one Saturday their parents called in the morning and sounded far away. A whistling sound in the background scared Kobi. She asked the Great Alighieri to please come home. He said it wasn't that simple. He called her little bunny.

Afterward, Grandmamma rocked her and reminded her their parents were going to be gone for a whole month longer, so they had to be patient. She kissed Kobi's head and said not to worry. She drove them to Monterey to watch the silly sea lions.

Their parents didn't call again.

Grandmamma said they'd run into bad weather, but it wouldn't amount to much because October wasn't storm season around Fiji and American Samoa. But in a few days, Kobi and Brook eavesdropped on a conversation Grandmamma was having with their half uncle. Grandmamma was crying and using words they didn't understand. That night, when Brook was snoring beside her, Kobi slipped out of bed.

A strip of light gleamed under the guest room door. Kobi heard Grandmamma's voice on the phone as she tip-toed past.

She made her way down the hall and slipped under her mother's desk into the hideaway. Using her flashlight, she found the magic words in the drawstring bag where she'd put them. She smoothed out the wrinkled ones and put the words written on yellow Post-its in two columns:

carillon	*fiddlesticks*
snapdragon	*razzmatazz*
squelch	*mayfly*
temporarily	*caribou*
honeysuckle	*freesia*
trillium	*phyllo bundle*
buoy	*dilettante*
veronica	*pantaloons*

She couldn't read most of them because she was only five, but they tingled with magic as she ran her fingers over them. She studied them. Why did one of the Post-its have two words? Did it mean phyllo bundle was extra powerful and to be used for the most important things, like bringing her parents home?

Kobi pressed her thumb against *phyllo bundle* and shut her eyes. She wanted the Great Alighieri to pull her close as they read *Mr. Popper's Penguins* together. She told them to come home. She *ordered* them to come home.

She waited. She didn't hear the key in the lock or hear the Great Alighieri call, "Where is everybody?"

She made two rows of orange Post-its. She touched each word and told her parents to come home.

iridescence	*Montpellier*
dimpling	*malleable*
scrambled	*frippery*
hogwash	*parsimonious*
	ragout

She spread out the last few Post-its—the ones written on neon green—and studied them.

lingua franca
Avanti!
buoy

Her parents were not home and it was getting stuffy in the hideaway.

She didn't know how to make the words work. She rearranged them. She put long words in one group, middle-sized words in another group. She tried saying some of the words, but they were hard.

She yanked her hair. *Why* hadn't her mother explained how to unleash the magic power?

Only one word had an exclamation point beside it. She ran her finger over the letters, sounding them out in her mind.

A-van-ti!

At that moment, that night almost five years ago, in the hideaway under her mother's desk in the San Francisco house, Kobi heard a rumbling sound as if stones were falling away from an opening. And there they were.

The sailboat listed in the sand, a jagged hole in its side. Bright stars. A bonfire. Her parents' shapes moving around the fire-light.

"Hey!" she called.

Her dad turned the spit where a chicken-like thing was roasting. Her mother tried to open a can of beans. Kobi slipped her hand into her dad's, but he moved it to poke the roasting thing with a sharp stick.

Her mother stood up and walked toward the surf. Kobi followed. At the edge of the water, her mother stood gazing into the distance as if she had turned to petri-fied wood. Her face glistened with tears.

★

Kobi wiped tears off her own face, hoping Mademoiselle hadn't noticed. But Mademoiselle was admiring the detail of Brook's drawing of the poor gentian. Sometimes Kobi wondered if she and Brook were really sisters. But of course they were. Sisters and best friends.

✳

After discovering that her parents were okay, she wanted to wake Brook and tell her. Brook would have been so happy. But Brook and Grandmamma didn't know her mother had given her magic words before she disappeared. Grandmamma might not believe Kobi. The magic might stop working if she told, because her mother had said it was a secret.

✳

Kobi stood back and looked at her painting. There was their house in San Francisco in the upper right corner. And Grandmamma walking from Paris on what looked like a hanging bridge but was really the cat's cradle, and of course Grandmamma hadn't really walked, but she had come. And she had stayed. And she kept them close and brought them back to Paris with her to wait. The storm and the boat with a gaping hole in its side took up a lot of space on the canvas. But something was missing from the canvas. Something to bind all the parts together.

Mademoiselle had taught them calligraphy, so Kobi decorated the left border of the painting with *iridescence*. That looked quite nice lettered vertically down the edge, and Mademoiselle would admire it because it was so Latinate. Kobi was half Latinate, in a way. Her Italian grandfather, whom she had visited when she was four, was handsome like the Great Alighieri. They hadn't been able to talk to each other very well, but Kobi loved the smell of the linen shop where her Italian grandparents flung out wide swaths of fabric on the cutting table for customers to see. That was how *iridescence* worked. It made a moment come alive. When she said *iridescence,* everything glowed around the edges. She could smell things, like the bolts of linen. She could hear and feel the *thunk* of the heavy bolt of fabric on the cutting board. *Iridescence* made a perfect left margin for her picture. She balanced it on the other side with *lingua franca,* which she had not yet learned how to use.

MONTPELLIER

THREE

*T*HAT evening, Mr. Gyver came to dinner. Grandmamma arranged seven cobalt-blue vases on the mantel below the Louis XV mirror. She began filling them with freesia. She filled the first one for her first husband, Kobi and Brook's grandfather, whom they never knew. She filled the next one for their mother and the Great Alighieri. The next one for Grandmamma's second husband, Mr. Mallory. The next for Grandmamma and Mr. Mallory's son, Wimbledon, their half uncle.

"We've never met him," Kobi said.

"Yes, we have," Brook said.

"No, we haven't."

"Yes, we have."

"Girls," Grandmamma said.

One freesia bouquet was for Brook. One was for Kobi.

"Who is the last one for?" Brook asked.

"For Leonard." Grandmamma smiled at Mr. Gyver, who smiled back.

"I'm entering a new phase of my life, girls," Grandmamma announced, looking both happy and anxious as she put the flowers in the last vase. "Leonard and I aren't getting any younger and we've decided to marry."

"Can we be bridesmaids?" Brook said.

Grandmamma laughed. "We're too old for all that. We'll be married at city hall in a few weeks while you girls are with your uncle Wim in Des Moines."

The last time Kobi had been separated from people she loved, it hadn't turned out well. "But we don't know him! Why can't we stay here?"

"Because Leonard and I are going to Beijing, where he is to receive an award, and then we will travel around the Far East for a while. It will be a honeymoon." Grandma's cheeks pinked up and she said, "Won't that be nice?"

"We could stay here with Madame Louise and Mademoiselle," Brook said. "This is our home."

Grandmamma kissed Brook's head. "Yes, it is. When we all return from our travels, Leonard will move here because this is your home. Going to the US will be an adventure. You'll get to know Wim. You'll experience an American school again after all these years."

Kobi remembered nothing about kindergarten except the time the Great Alighieri came to visit.

"We'll all be back here for Christmas," Grandmamma said. "Together."

She kissed Mr. Gyver's head then, and he caught her hand.

"You are fine girls," he said. "I will try to be a good stepgrandfather."

Kobi liked Mr. Gyver, and she liked for Grandmamma to be happy, but she worried about being apart. *Caribou,* she said to herself when Grandmamma sank into her chair and lifted her wineglass to Mr. Gyver. *Caribou, I love you. You can go away but you have to come back.* It worked to bring Grandmamma back from dining with friends, from outings with Mr. Gyver, from the hairdresser, from visiting with the concierge. It would bring her back from the Far East.

✷

Grandmamma said that because of Mr. Gyver's prize, there wasn't a moment to be wasted. Thus, Kobi and Brook and Grandmamma found themselves in the Paris airport only two weeks later.

Grandmamma had worry lines as she searched the crowd for Mr. Gyver. He should have picked them up at the apartment and brought them to Charles de Gaulle. But he hadn't come and didn't answer his phone, so finally they had called a taxi. And here they were in line, and would soon be sucked through the security gate.

Grandmamma would fret all the way across the Atlantic if she didn't see Mr. Gyver before they got on the plane. She tried telephoning him once again. "He'd forget his head if it weren't screwed on."

Brook fiddled with the zipper pulls on her carry-on. When they were all perfectly centered, she turned to Kobi. She ran her finger from the tip of Kobi's nose up Kobi's forehead to the barrette that held back Kobi's growing-out bangs. And then she used her hands to measure the distance from Kobi's ears to the barrette.

People were staring. Kobi wanted to push Brook's hands away, but she didn't because Brook was trying to keep any more people from disappearing.

Montpellier. The word echoed nicely in Kobi's head, like a shout in a cave. *Montpellier—ellier—ellier.* Which was probably why it was a good word for big, cavernous places like airports and cathedrals.

"There's Mr. Gyver!" Brook cried, pointing.

The worry lines between Grandmamma's eyes vanished as Mr. Gyver waved from the crowd.

Kobi smiled.

Mr. Gyver was out of breath when he reached them. ". . . Oh, Amelia, I overslept . . . misplaced my telephone . . . sorry." He kissed Grandmamma on each cheek, making her look like a flower that had been watered. "And I am sorry if you girls were worried," he said, turning to them.

Kobi threw her arms around him. He smelled like toothpaste and the little brown cigarettes he was always trying to give up.

They were almost to the security gate. Mr. Gyver gave

Kobi and Brook quick kisses. "See you at Christmas." He gave Grandmamma another peck. "See you Sunday, my dear."

And then they removed their shoes and placed their belongings in a tub on the moving belt.

The security machine behaved perfectly when Grandmamma and Brook went through. But it squawked at Kobi, making her heart nearly leap out of her throat and making everybody look at her. A security guard told her to lift her arms and then ran a wand around her body.

"Do you have something in your pocket?" he asked.

The key.

Kobi nodded.

He told Kobi to place whatever it was in the bin.

Grandmamma's frown warned Kobi not to make a fuss, but things could happen to a small key in a busy airport. The key caught the light as she placed it in the bin. *Dimpling,* she breathed as the bin disappeared into the maw of the security machine. *Dimpling,* she said to herself as the guard waved her through the gate. *Dimpling,* she whispered as she waited for the bin to reappear. And there was the key! Kobi dropped it in her pocket.

Awhile later, when the plane leveled off above the clouds, Brook said, "Tighten your seat belt in case we hit air pockets. And finish your orange juice in case you have to go to the bathroom. You can't go while we're landing."

"But we don't land for hours."

"But we might land *unexpectedly.* Fix your hair clip, too.

Hair in your eyes can make you blind."

Kobi's hair did keep falling over her face, which made Grandmamma cross. So Kobi smoothed it and reset the clip in the exact center to keep everybody happy. She had to admit she could see better—though there was nothing to see except the seats in front of her.

Brook took the magazines and information cards out of the seat pocket. She put them back so they were centered, smaller things in front of larger things. Then she did it again. And again. Kobi knew better than to interfere. If Brook had decided she needed to organize them five times, and Kobi interrupted her, Brook would have to start over.

So Kobi shut her eyes. The plane droned, seeming barely to be moving. Wrapped in the hum, she tried to relax. When her toes were nicely limp, she said *Avanti!*

Silvery waves broke on the shore. Gulls circled in the wind. Her mother knelt on the beach, washing clothes in the surf. On a thorny bush, she had pinned a shirt to dry. It was the one she'd worn when she waved goodbye the day she and the Great Alighieri sailed out of San Francisco Bay. The shirt was faded and ragged. The Great Alighieri was dragging a net into the surf.

Kobi tried to make them understand that they needed to hurry home.

SNAPDRAGON

FOUR

*T*HEY had a brief stop at O'Hare—long enough to eat what Grandmamma called *famous* Chicago hot dogs—before they made their way to the gate.

Brook stared at the Chicago hot dog when it was put in front of her. "Something's wrong with it," she said, pointing to the strange, curving X shape of the ends.

"It's cooked in the *cervelat* style," Grandmamma said, "but try it. You'll like it."

Brook took a cautious bite.

"While you're here, remember not to remark on differences too much," Grandmamma said. "It's rude."

"Why has Uncle Wim never come to visit us in France?" Kobi asked, wiping mustard off her fingers. It didn't look or taste like mustard, though Grandmamma assured her it was. *American* mustard.

"Wim doesn't like to fly," Grandmamma said. "It's difficult for him. Especially long transatlantic trips."

"Why have we never gone to see him?" Brook asked.

Grandma dabbed her lips with her napkin and sighed. "Families are complicated."

"Do you not like Uncle Wim?" Kobi asked. "Because if you don't, maybe we shouldn't stay with him."

"Of course I like Wim!" Grandmamma exclaimed.

"Does he not like you?" Kobi asked. That was hard for her to believe.

"Parents and their grown children don't always agree," Grandmamma said. "But don't worry. You're going to have an adventure. And it's just for a little while."

★

Their plane landed in Des Moines on time at 4:45.

Kobi spotted her half uncle, whom she recognized from pictures, in the crowd at the bottom of the escalator. He wore a T-shirt that said YOU CAN'T BEAT A WOMAN.

"What does that mean?" Brook asked Kobi as, from a few steps behind them, Grandmamma called, "Wave, girls!"

They waved.

He waved back.

As they got off the escalator, Grandmamma kissed Uncle Wim's cheek and he hugged her, but Kobi thought they acted like each thought the other didn't want to.

"Wim, you remember your nieces," she said, turning to Kobi and Brook.

"Hello, nieces," he said.

"This is your uncle Wim," Grandmamma chirped to Brook and Kobi. "You three are going to get along famously!"

One of his eyebrows went up. He slung Grandmamma's carry-on over one shoulder and Brook's and Kobi's over the other. On the way through the busy terminal, he stared straight ahead as if leading the way to the baggage carousel were dangerous work.

Grandmamma and Brook saw a restroom and detoured. Kobi went with Uncle Wim to get their luggage.

The carousel began to turn as they arrived. Beside her, Uncle Wim waited, stiff as a nutcracker.

She asked him what the message on his T-shirt meant.

He glanced down. "Oh." He made a fist and looked mean. "You can't *beat* a woman, and you can't beat a *woman*." He made a kind of goofy face. "Get it?"

She shook her head.

He pulled out the front of his shirt and stared at the message as if he didn't understand what was not to get. When the conveyor belt began to spit out luggage, he looked relieved.

"The pink ones are mine," Kobi said. "The purple ones are Brook's."

Uncle Wim began to grab suitcases off the carousel, piling them on a cart. When no more pink or purple appeared, he looked at the stack of luggage as high as his shoulders. "Surely this can't be everything."

"Except for my footlocker," Kobi said, pointing. She patted her pocket to make sure the key was there.

✱

Houses shaded by trees lined the streets. Kobi watched Uncle Wim's eyebrows in the mirror. They were talkative like her mother's.

He caught her eye. "What's in your footlocker?"

"Things."

Grandmamma cleared her throat.

"There's nothing alive, is there? Nothing else I'm going to have to feed and take care of?"

"No!" Kobi said. She thought his eyebrows said he was joking, but she wasn't sure.

"I hope there's nothing *dead* in there."

"Never mind, Wim," Grandmamma said firmly.

"What's that?" Brook cried.

Kobi turned to look where Brook was pointing. A colorful stack of chairs made a pillar in front of a little stone house. At the top of the column, a red chair perched at a tilt, one fancy leg stuck out like a can can dancer's.

Uncle Wim pulled to the curb.

A woman in cutoffs was pushing a lawn mower along the bank in front of the house. She wore boots and her bare legs were peppered with bits of grass. She stopped mowing and came to Uncle Wim's window, her eyes hidden behind sunglasses.

"Hello, Amelia," she said.

"Sally Hancock," Grandmamma said, a chill in her voice.

"Meet new fans of the chairs," Uncle Wim said. He tilted his head toward Kobi and Brook. "Kids, this is my friend Sally. And those are her mother's chairs."

Brook asked, "How did your mother get them up so high?"

"With difficulty."

"Aren't you afraid they'll fall over?"

The woman laughed. "That's most of the point."

"But don't they get wet when it rains?" Brook asked. "And what about bird poop?"

"Brook, it's *art*," Grandmamma said in a voice icy enough to fog the windows.

Sally Hancock said, "It's an installation. My mother is a sculptor."

"Our mother is a writer," Kobi said. "And our dad is a magician."

Uncle Wim's head swiveled and he looked at her as if she had begun barking.

"How *is* Patricia?" Grandmamma asked Sally Hancock.

"Mom's fine," she said.

They talked a little longer and then Uncle Wim drove on. On a narrow, shady street, they passed a brick church. The bells in the tower, which Uncle Wim called a carillon, pealed out a song.

"How do you spell that?" Kobi asked.

"*C-a-r-i-l-l-o-n.*"

As she thought, she realized it was one of the magic words she hadn't yet found the use of.

"Why did you ask?"

"I just wondered."

Soon Uncle Wim turned into a gravel alley and stopped.

When Kobi got out of the car, the breeze dried her sweaty legs and she felt more hopeful. Inside would be icy lemonade, a cool bath, clean pj's, and a comfy bed.

Uncle Wim's house was white with fancy cutouts around the front porch. The second story disappeared into the trees. The back porch sagged and the sidewalk was uneven.

"Wim, why do you live in a place like this—"

Uncle Wim's hand went up as if he were stopping traffic. Grandmamma sighed.

Uncle Wim unlocked the door to the back porch and held it open for them.

As Kobi stepped into the dim, hot kitchen, she felt a long way from home.

In the dining room, a chandelier furry with dust hung from a high ceiling. Kobi waited for Grandmamma to ask where they would eat, because there was no table. No sideboard. No petit point dining room chairs.

Grandmamma shook her head. "If you would buy some nice antiques, Wim . . ."

"Ah. Furniture." Uncle Wim opened his mouth again as if to say something about furniture. Then closed it.

In the living room, newspapers, a pizza box, crumpled socks, and a T-shirt were scattered around a brown recliner. The room looked like the nest of some large animal that pawed and snorted in its sleep. A huge black couch with saggy cushions crouched in the opposite corner.

Kobi glanced at Grandmamma for assurance that she wouldn't abandon them here.

"The last people left the couch," Uncle Wim explained. "I guess they couldn't get it out."

"Then how did they get it in?" Brook asked.

Uncle Wim fixed her with a look.

Grandmamma *wouldn't* leave them here, would she? Yet Kobi had learned that grown-ups sometimes did selfish things. Like set off on long ocean voyages without their children.

"And this would be the foyer," Grandmamma said, a line of sweat trickling down her powdered cheek.

In the foyer, a carved staircase went up to a landing, where a stained-glass window glowed. Then the staircase turned on itself and disappeared into the shadows.

"Follow me, ladies," Uncle Wim said, his voice echoing.

The farther up they went, the hotter Kobi got.

At the top, Uncle Wim said, "Bet you've never seen such

a big bathroom." He opened a door that squealed on its hinges.

They could stand straight only in the middle of the room. The rest of the ceiling sloped almost to the floor. Uncle Wim switched on a fan, which stirred the air. At the end of the narrow room hung the head of an animal with large, pointy horns.

Brook screamed.

"It's an oryx," Uncle Wim said. "The eyes light up. The last people left that too."

"Let's see the guest bedroom," Grandmamma said, worry in her voice.

Uncle Wim led them down the hall. "There's a little porch out that door," he explained, pointing. "And this is the guest room."

Sunshine poured through several windows. The white paint of the woodwork shone, and a bay window had a cozy seat. Gold-and-white-striped paper covered the walls. White curtains billowed in the breeze. A squirrel sat on a branch only a few feet away, flicking its tail. It was not at all a bad room.

"But where's our bed?" Brook asked. "A bedroom has to have a *bed*. That's what the word means."

Uncle Wim fixed her with that look again as if he didn't like smarty children, and then he pointed to boxes against the wall. He glanced at Grandmamma, his face red.

She gasped, "*Still. In. The. Box?* Wimbledon!"

"Well, Mom, it's not like I had a lot of notice."

Kobi said *Snapdragon* to herself halfheartedly, which was probably why it didn't work. *Snapdragon* was a foot-stomping magic word. A command. She used it to conjure the bill in cafés, for example, when Grandmamma was getting impatient and cranky. Of course, it never worked when she tried to use it selfishly, but Brook and Grandmamma wanted a bed too—though perhaps not as much as she.

SQUELCH

FIVE

*K*OBI was as hot and sticky as one of Madame Louise's pound cakes. She stripped off her dress. "Hurry *up!*" she told Brook. "It's my turn."

Brook stood in the claw-footed tub, stooping to avoid banging her head on the sloping ceiling. "I need a mat. Look around, would you? Maybe there's one in the closet." She pointed at the little door under the eaves.

Kobi peered inside. The closet was empty except for one towel. "There's nothing in here but one towel, and Grand-mamma will need that."

Brook dripped indignantly. "We *each* get *one towel*?"

"Use our dirty clothes to drip on." With her foot, Kobi slid her dress to the side of the tub.

Brook stepped out, her wet feet leaving marks on the dress.

Kobi climbed in.

"Nasty!" Brook cried. "Tell me you—"

But Kobi slid under. It had taken half an hour to fill the long tub because the water came out in a twisty little trickle the size of her pinky. Kobi would be a melted blob on the bathroom floor before the tub filled again.

She held her breath underwater as long as she could, listening to pinging and burbling. Finally, she came up for air.

She relaxed against the tub's sloping back. It was getting dark outside and the little windows along the floor didn't let in much light.

"Maybe we should turn on the oryx," she said.

"You know I don't like light-up eyes."

"You don't like dark places, either."

"Fine," Brook said in a too-tired-to-argue voice. "How do I turn it on?"

"There's got to be a switch."

Brook climbed onto the sink and felt around. "This is very creepy."

Suddenly, the room lit up, making both girls scream. The oryx moved, Kobi was quite sure. It shifted its head and pinned her in its bright gaze. *Squelch!*

"Girls?" called Grandmamma. "What's going on?"

Squelch. Squelch. Squelch, squelch, squelch.

Kobi stared at the animal. It looked calmer now. Less

vicious. But she didn't want it watching her with its weird eyes. "Turn it off!"

"I don't know how! I don't even know why it went on."

"Then throw my dress over it!"

Once the oryx was wrapped in Kobi's white eyelet dress, it made a moonlight glow. And except for the horns, it didn't look vicious. Kobi's heart slowed down. She thought it was safe to get out of the tub. Using her big toe, she pulled the plug and let the bathwater run very slowly down the drain.

✳

Kobi settled into Uncle Wim's bed with Grandmamma and Brook. Uncle Wim said he would sleep in his recliner. The closet door was open and she saw khakis hanging on a rod. Between two windows stood a tall metal bookshelf crammed with books and stacks of folders. There was a framed picture, too, but Kobi couldn't make out who was in it. Bugs tapped the screens and insects screeched in the trees.

Grandmamma turned off the lamp. "Maybe the bugs will settle down now," she said as the carillon struck the hour. She yawned. "Nine o'clock. Four in the morning Paris time. No wonder we're exhausted." She drew them close. "I want you to enjoy this adventure, girls. Wim takes getting used to, I'll admit. But I'm very proud of my son. If everybody were like him, the world would be a better place. Don't forget that."

Maybe Grandmamma understood how living in an

empty house without enough towels made the world a better place, but Kobi did not. She yawned.

Soon Grandmamma began to snore gently. Brook mumbled something and turned over. Kobi rolled on her side, her back against Grandmamma's softness.

She fell asleep in the middle of *Avanti!*

✴

Birdsong woke her. The dead weight of Brook's arm lay across her waist. Grandmamma was already up.

In the bathroom, Kobi started to say *Squelch* but decided the oryx wasn't so scary this morning. She listened for sounds of Grandmamma or Uncle Wim, but all she heard was a dog barking.

She was wrapped in a blanket of tiredness, and she thought about crawling back into bed, but she went to the bookshelf instead. She looked at the picture of a beautiful lady holding a pudgy toddler in her arms. A teenage girl beside her glared at the camera. Kobi had seen similar pictures in Grandmamma's albums. It was a picture of Grandmamma, Uncle Wim, and Kobi and Brook's mother.

The cover of the book beside it showed a chicken strolling through a pretty garden. The title was *Free-Range Chicken Gardens: How to Create a Beautiful Chicken-Friendly Yard*. There were a lot of garden books on the shelf. *The Organic Gardener's Handbook of Natural Pest and Disease Control; Mini Farming: Learn How to Create an Organic Garden in Your Backyard.* She went down the hall. On the right, in the room that would be theirs, she studied the boxes. Twin beds. Somebody should have told Uncle Wim that she and Brook slept together. And somebody should have told Grandmamma that abandoning granddaughters in America with a half uncle, two beds, and three towels was a bad idea.

Across the hall, she discovered a tiny room with two tall, narrow windows. Faded blue paper with shiny little stars covered the walls. Her footlocker sat on the floor. Five years ago, it had gotten dinged up on the trip from San Francisco to Paris. And it now had a new scratch in the shape of a lightning bolt on one side. Kobi tried the clasp to make sure it was locked.

She went outside onto the porch. It was about the same size as the stone balcony of Grandmamma's apartment. But this porch was wooden, and the paint was peeling. In Paris, when she stood on the balcony, she looked down on the awnings of Monsieur le Bault's bakery across the street. Here, she looked down at grass growing through a broken sidewalk.

The smell of coffee drifted up from below. Uncle Wim said, "Did you get any sleep?"

"Alas, no," Grandmamma said, her voice sounding tired. The porch swing made creaking noises. "I'm getting old, Wim. And some days, I feel so tired."

"You're not old, Mom!"

"And it's killing me to leave the girls," Grandmamma said.

"They'll be fine. It's for a few months. I'll take them shopping for school supplies on Sunday and they'll start school Monday. Then they'll be too busy to get homesick."

"Maybe. But they've led quiet lives, Wim. Remember that. They've been around mainly tutors and old people."

"You're not having second thoughts, are you? Not after you brought them all this way."

Kobi held her breath and squeezed her eyes shut. It seemed to be taking Grandmamma a long time to answer.

Malleable. That word often worked to help people decide to do the right thing, which, in this case, Kobi felt sure, was to take them back to Paris.

Grandmamma sighed. "I guess I am having second thoughts, Wim."

Kobi let out her breath and opened her eyes. Yes.

"But they need to get to know you. And you need to get to know them. And you and I need to be a little closer. Just in case."

Just in case? Kobi shivered as if something had run its icy fingers through her hair.

"In case what, Mom?"

"Oh, Wim. They've been scarred by what happened. Poor Brook works with a therapist for her OCD, but I'm worried . . ."

A car with a loud muffler went by, setting off the dogs in the neighborhood and blanking out what Grandmamma and Uncle Wim were saying for a while.

". . . the therapist says when the time is right, she'll be able to accept what happened and start to remember. But it's best not to push. Not to insist."

What did Brook not remember?

Kobi remembered everything. Every single detail. Most of all, she remembered being so happy to find the magic words that let her discover her parents safe on the island. She wished she could tell Brook and Grandmamma, but her mother had said the words were serious magic. *Secret* serious magic.

SCRAMBLED

SIX

*T*HEY sat around the wobbly little table in the kitchen. Grandmamma brushed Kobi's hair out of her eyes and tucked it behind her ear.

Brook scowled at the jibbled-up stuff Uncle Wim was scooping onto their paper plates.

"Your uncle makes *scrambled* pancakes. It's his specialty!" Grandmamma announced in a bright voice.

"Why would you scramble a pancake?" Brook grumbled.

Uncle Wim placed syrup and a jar of peanut butter on the table. "Why would you scramble an egg?"

"Because scrambled eggs are good," Brook said.

Scrambled was one of the words Kobi's mother had given her. Kobi had tried it for all sorts of things. Making the little dog in the dress shop let her pet him. She knew he would feel better if she petted him. Making things fall off Grandmamma's schedule so she would go on the field trip to the Louvre with Kobi and Brook and the other homeschooled kids. Grandmamma would have more fun doing that than going to a boring meeting.

Uncle Wim sat down, jiggling the table and sloshing milk out of Kobi's glass. For an instant, she waited for Madame Louise to clean it up. And then Uncle Wim thrust a roll of paper towels at her.

She blotted up the mess.

"You have to eat these the right way." Uncle Wim smeared globs of peanut butter over the lumps and then poured thick syrup on them. He looked at Kobi, waiting for her to copy him.

She drizzled syrup over the lumps on her paper plate and picked up her fork. Peanut butter did not go with pancakes.

"Peanut butter is part of the package," Uncle Wim said, adding a few dollops to the mess on her plate without her permission. Then he swirled everything together until it looked, as Madame Louise said, like something from the seventh stomach of a cow.

Kobi glared at Uncle Wim. Now she had nothing to eat.

A gallon of milk sweated in the middle of the table. Madame Louise put the milk in a pitcher and the pitcher on a plate. And the table didn't jiggle.

Grandmamma said with determined cheerfulness, "Oh,

Wim. You should patent these pancakes." She blotted her mouth on a paper towel.

Madame Louise used *linen* napkins and *china* plates. And pretty place mats.

Kobi took a bite of the disgusting-looking food only because hunger moved her hand. *Scrambled,* she said to herself, hoping maybe . . . The gooey stuff tasted . . .

. . . so delicious Kobi shut her eyes and held it on her tongue. And then she mashed it against the roof of her mouth and made a humming sound. *Scrambled!*

"Wim, promise me you'll get the upstairs plumbing fixed so the tub will fill in less than an hour," Grandmamma said. "Otherwise the girls will spend all their time trying to bathe."

Uncle Wim's face turned red slowly, starting at his neck and rising to his hair.

"Ding-dong," somebody called from the back door.

"Yo!" Uncle Wim called.

The lawn-mowing lady from yesterday stepped into the room. The toolbox made the muscles in her arms bulge. "I thought you might need an extra pair of hands with the beds." She plunked the metal box onto the counter. A sticker on it read REAL WOMEN FIX DRIPS.

"That's kind of you, Sally Hancock," Grandmamma said stiffly.

Why did Grandmamma always use Sally Hancock's last name? Was that what they did in America?

"Want some breakfast first?" Uncle Wim asked, smiling at her.

Sally Hancock shook her head. "No thanks." She poured a mug of coffee and leaned against the counter.

Kobi wanted a bed to sleep in, but she was not going to leave one bite of the scrambled pancakes uneaten.

"Well," Sally Hancock said. "Who's good at following directions for assembling beds?"

"I am!" Brook waved her hand in the air. "I am an extremely well-organized person."

Kobi tried not to roll her eyes. That was one way to describe her sister.

"I'll go on and get started," Sally Hancock said, picking up her toolbox and clumping through the empty dining room. "Come when you're ready."

Brook asked to be excused, and soon Kobi heard scooting and bumping sounds overhead.

"I didn't know the upstairs tub was slow to fill," he said to Kobi, as if she were the one who'd asked him to fix it. "I've always used the shower down here." He pointed to the little bathroom off the kitchen.

His shirt pocket quacked like a duck and he looked at his cell phone. He went to the back porch, where Kobi heard him talking.

She couldn't stop stuffing herself with scrambled pancakes. Between bites, she gulped cold milk from her sweaty glass. She had never had a more delicious breakfast.

Against the light, the shape of Grandmamma's head showed through her hair. The sudden knot in Kobi's throat made her put down her fork.

Her grandmother sipped her coffee and was silent.

Uncle Wim came back into the kitchen. "I need to take a woman and her children to the Domestic Violence Shelter."

Grandmamma looked surprised. "But it's Saturday."

"I'm on call."

Grandmamma stood and smoothed the front of her robe. "Then we'll keep the home fires burning, won't we, Kobi?"

This would be the last morning Kobi would see her grandmother for a long time.

As if Grandmamma had read her thoughts, she said, "Everything will be fine."

After Uncle Wim left, Kobi asked, "What's the Domestic Violence Shelter?"

Grandmamma sighed. "I believe it's a place for women and children to go when someone is hurting them at home."

"Why would someone do that?"

Grandmamma took a deep breath. "Wim has always liked to help people. His father was the same way. But Wimbledon could have been a doctor. Or a diplomat. Or even a teacher. There are many ways of helping people. I don't know why he had to be a social worker."

That wasn't the question Kobi had asked, but maybe Grandmamma had answered the question Kobi had been wondering about. Uncle Wim didn't like Grandmamma telling him what to do because he was grown up. And Grandmamma was happiest when people did what she wanted.

"Is Sally Hancock Uncle Wim's girlfriend?"

"Oh!" Grandmamma exclaimed as if somebody had stepped on her bare toes. "Heavens no. Why would you think that?"

Kobi didn't know, except she had observed that older people had girlfriends and boyfriends. And fiancés.

"Oh no, no, no," Grandmamma said. "Sally Hancock is not at all my son's type. Plus, she's years older."

"Why do you use her last name?"

Grandmamma shot Kobi a look that warned about asking personal questions.

Kobi dropped the subject. But how did Grandmamma expect them to live here without information?

★

After the beds were assembled, Sally Hancock left. Soon Uncle Wim returned from helping the family who had been hurt, and they went to the mall. Grandmamma found fluffy comforters and pillows for their new beds. She bought a lamp with a fringe of beads that twinkled when Kobi ran her fingers around the edge. Grandmamma bought piles of thick striped towels. She bought a bath mat shaped like a zebra, pretty soap, bubble bath, and toothbrush cups with fish on them. Uncle Wim trailed along, making trips to the car with their bags.

Finally, they ate a hurried meal at the food court. Then they rushed home and washed the new sheets and put them on the beds and set up the lamp and snipped tags off towels and packed Grandmamma's bag and rushed to the airport.

The airport lights turned the twilight a weird color, as if they were on another planet, which was how Kobi felt.

Grandmamma said, "Drop me off, Wim. Everyone's exhausted."

Uncle Wim pulled to the curb and they all got out.

"Here's your carry-on," Brook said, placing it at Grandmamma's feet. "Do you have your passport and boarding pass?"

Grandmamma patted her purse.

"You should actually *check*," Brook said.

Grandmamma got out the two documents. She looked about ready to cry.

"Do you have your sleep mask and your eyedrops?" Brook asked.

Grandmamma nodded.

"You should check."

Kobi noticed the way Uncle Wim's eyebrows moved as he watched Brook.

"I have what I need, honey." Grandmamma kissed Uncle Wim on the cheek.

Uncle Wim hugged her. "Take care of yourself, Mom. And don't worry."

"You're a good son, Wim," Grandmamma said, hugging him back.

Kobi, Brook, and Grandmamma fell into each other's arms. Kobi pressed her face into Grandmamma's silk shirt. She could feel Grandmamma's heart racing and Grandmamma's arms tightening around them. Too quickly, Grandmamma stepped away and walked through the doors.

Kobi hoped she would look back and wave, but she didn't. Kobi was going to call, "Give my love to Mr. Gyver." But Grandmamma rushed into the crowd. *Caribou. I love you.*

They were quiet in the car. Finally, Uncle Wim asked if they'd like to eat at the mall again.

Kobi glanced at Brook, who barely shook her head. "No. Thank you," Kobi said.

Kobi was lonely already. She could tell by the look on Brook's face that her sister was, too.

"Girls, you have to eat. If you don't, I'll get in trouble."

"Could we have real food?" Brook asked.

"What do you mean?" Uncle Wim asked.

On hot evenings like this, Madame Louise gave them *vichyssoise*, a delicious cold potato soup. And bread, crusty on the outside, soft as clouds on the inside. And little wedges of cheese, crumbly and salty. And juicy pears from the silver bowl on the dining room table.

"How about scrambled pancakes?" Uncle Wim suggested.

Kobi nodded. Brook rolled her eyes.

★

Before they went to bed, they put their luggage in two identical stacks in front of the bay window so Brook would stop
worrying that something terrible would happen if the room
wasn't symmetrical.

Kobi got between the new sheets, but she couldn't sleep.
She missed having her sister beside her in bed.

A car cruised past, sending thudding music into the night.

"Why didn't Uncle Wim buy one big bed?" Brook asked.

"Maybe he didn't have enough money. I think he's unfortunate."

"Does one big bed cost more than two little ones?" Brook
asked.

"Probably."

Kobi stared into the darkness. The sound of Uncle Wim's
TV drifted up. He was in his creaky recliner right below
them.

"Do you think Grandmamma is missing us?" Kobi asked.
She hated to think of Grandmamma sitting by strangers.

"Yes," Brook said.

Kobi heard the TV go off and heard Uncle Wim on the
phone, but she couldn't make out the words.

"I'll bet he's talking to his girlfriend," Brook said.

"She's not his girlfriend. I asked Grandmamma."

"Well, Grandmamma doesn't like her," Brook said. "So
we shouldn't, either."

"It would serve Grandmamma right if we did," Kobi
said.

Brook said, "We mustn't be mad at Grandmamma . . ." She was silent until she exploded into sobs. ". . . or she might not come back!"

Kobi scrambled out of her bed, taking her pillow with her. Brook turned away, yanking the sheet over her head, but Kobi wrapped her in a hug. "Grandmamma will be back," she whispered, but her own eyes suddenly flooded with tears. *Caribou, caribou.*

Finally, Brook uncovered her head. After a while, Kobi felt Brook breathing evenly and one of her feet twitched.

Kobi didn't hear Uncle Wim's voice anymore. Actually, she didn't hear a single inside sound. No TV. No banging of pipes that went along with water running anyplace in the house. No recliner creaking. Surely he wouldn't go off and leave them alone.

Brook jerked awake. "Kobi?"

"What?" Kobi whispered.

"I have to count the stripes on the wallpaper."

Kobi groaned and buried her face in the pillow.

The lamp went on and after a while Kobi heard it being scooted. Then the lamp went off and Brook got back into bed.

"There are thirty-one stripes," she whispered. "But I put the lamp in front of one, so it doesn't count. That leaves thirty, which can be divided evenly by two, three, and five . . ."

Kobi turned the sound of Brook's voice down and slipped away with *Avanti!*

Her parents were bedding down, too. They were high in the tree house. Beneath the stars, the damaged sailboat bobbed in the cove.

Her mother unrolled a mat she had woven from grass. Her dad yanked a cord and a curtain of mosquito netting dropped around them. They snuggled like Brook and Kobi were snuggling. A chorus of insects sang in the trees.

"Good night, Beatrice, my love," the Great Alighieri whispered. "Good night, bunnies."

"Good night, Al," their mother whispered. "Good night, my babies. Sleep well."

"Good night," Kobi said, knowing they couldn't hear her.

FRIPPERY

SEVEN

$\mathcal{S}$HE woke up to sunshine and Brook's pokes. Kobi yanked the sheet over her face. Brook tugged it away.

"Get up," Brook said, trying to sit on Kobi. "I'm lonesome."

Kobi groaned and sat up. Brook's purple luggage was open and stuff was scattered everywhere.

"I have this idea," Brook announced. "We could turn the room across the hall into our closet." She picked up a pair of fur-lined boots and a woolly hat with earflaps. "We can leave these winter things packed away and stack the suitcases neatly along the wall. Then . . ."

Kobi's stomach growled so loudly Brook stopped talking.

"Let's have breakfast first," Kobi said.

"Can't. Uncle Wim is outside mowing."

Hunger was jabbing holes in Kobi's stomach. She helped Madame Louise cook all the time. "I can make pancakes."

Downstairs, they found the skillet and a box of mix on the counter from the night before.

"Read the directions," Kobi said.

One of Brook's eyebrows went up. "Heat the skillet—"

Kobi turned a knob, but nothing happened. In Madame Louise's kitchen, the stove burner twinkled immediately into a gentle ring of flame.

She leaned forward to look. Nothing. *Snapdragon!*

Fwooom!

Kobi leapt back, her face scorched. Her hair made a crinkling noise.

Uncle Wim strode in, putting his phone in his shirt pocket. "Text from Mom. She touched down at Charles de Gaulle. She sends her love." He sniffed. "Smells like somebody is cooking a chicken with its feathers on." His gaze landed on Kobi. His eyebrows sprang into the air.

Uncle Wim crossed the room and turned off the stove. When he finally looked at them, his face was red. "Mom will kill me if I let anything happen to you. So from now on. No. Using. The stove." His voice rose. His eyes drilled into Kobi. "Got it?"

She nodded.

His eyes went to Brook.

She nodded and said in a small voice, "But Kobi was hungry. And *I* didn't use the stove."

Kobi glared at Brook.

Uncle Wim put his hands over his face as if, when he looked again, they would have disappeared. "Get dressed," he said. "We'll see what can be done about the hair."

They drove through a fast-food place on the way to wherever they were going, but Kobi couldn't eat the strange pale thing on a bun that came wrapped in warm, damp paper. When she sniffed it, it smelled like her dead hair. She left it lying on the seat. No amount of magic could make it edible.

★

At Quick Snips, Kobi tried not to look in the mirror.

"What happened?" the lady asked, pumping the chair up with her foot.

"I was making pancakes."

The lady shook her head. "Kids." She began spraying Kobi's head with icy water. Kobi closed her eyes, holding back tears, listening to the sound of long hair like her mother's sliding down the plastic cape.

"Have a look," the lady said after a while.

Kobi opened her eyes. A sad boy with a long neck and big ears stared at her.

"When I was a kid," the lady said, letting the chair down, "there was this model, Twiggy. She was skinny as a twig and she had a haircut like yours. For a few years, girls wanted *boy cuts,* as we called them then. Maybe you'll bring the style back."

Kobi couldn't say anything. The knot in her throat was too huge.

✳

In the car, Uncle Wim gave them their school supply lists. Kobi stared at the words. She couldn't think without her hair.

"We'll go to the mall," Uncle Wim said. "Sally gave me coupons."

"Why are our lists on different-colored paper?" Brook asked.

"Different schools, different lists," Uncle Wim said, stopping at a light.

"*Different schools?*" they cried.

"Kobi goes to Horace Mann Elementary and Brook goes to Lincoln Middle School."

"But Grandmamma said we'd go to the *same school*," Brook said. "The *same school*," she repeated loudly as if Uncle Wim might not understand English.

"Well, I don't know why she'd think that, since you're in different grades. The schools here are K through five and six through eight."

"I want to talk to Grandmamma," Brook said. "Right now."

Uncle Win sighed and handed his phone over the seat back.

When Grandmamma answered and Brook spilled out the terrible news, whatever Grandmamma said made Brook's face crumple. She thrust the phone at Kobi.

Malleable, Kobi breathed, taking the phone. She wasn't using the magic power selfishly. It was for Brook, too. It had almost worked yesterday for getting Grandmamma to do the right thing and take them back to Paris with her.

"Will you please tell Uncle Wim to move Brook to my school?" she asked. "It won't matter what grade we're in for a few months." *Malleable.*

Kobi heard background noise as if Grandmamma were in a cavernous place. Maybe *Montpellier* would be a better word. *Montpellier.*

"I'm going through customs now, sweetheart," Grandmamma said in a breaking-up voice. "But we'll work it out so you girls can be together. We may not get it worked out by tomorrow, so be brave for a couple of days, okay?"

Kobi didn't want to be separated from Brook for even one day, but she said "Okay" and handed the phone to Uncle Wim. "Grandmamma says we'll work it out. But not by tomorrow."

Brook crossed her arms. "Then we won't go to school tomorrow."

Uncle Wim glanced at them in the mirror, his brows in a no-nonsense line. "You *have* to go to school tomorrow because I have to go to work."

Brook sniffed and turned to stare out the window. After a while, she said, "You should have a housekeeper to watch us."

Uncle Wim barked a laugh. His neck turned red. Kobi felt sorry for him. He would probably have a housekeeper *and* furniture if he were more fortunate.

Temporarily. She used that word when she saw pe
the streets of Paris who Grandmamma said were u
nate. She could never tell for sure if the magic work
she hoped it did.

"Grandmamma can hire a housekeeper if you ca
ford one," Brook said.

Uncle Wim's eyes in the mirror turned cold. "No
you. It will be good for you to live like normal kids
change."

Kobi didn't want to live like a real kid if it mean
ing separated from her sister. She tried to swallow the a1
at her parents for going off on a sailing trip, and at Gr
mamma for going off on a wedding trip.

✳

As they traipsed from store to store buying school suppli
Kobi's naked neck and ears tingled. And they turned hot a
red even though she told them not to. People stared.

At lunch in the food court, Brook arranged her four cra
rangoons around the edge of her plate, the little cup of sauc
in the middle. She picked up each rangoon, bit off a corne1
and placed it back on the plate.

Uncle Wim watched. Kobi was glad he didn't say anything. After a while, he turned to Kobi. "You remind me of
your mother with that haircut," he said.

Her mother had waves and waves of beautiful hair. *Abun-
dant* hair, their dad said. One day on the island, he carved a
wooden comb out of a tree root a wild boar unearthed.

"When I was about four, Bea went to the mall one day and came home with a haircut like yours, except it was a little more spiky. And get this." He paused for drama. "She had a safety pin in her ear."

"Not possible," Brook said, biting a corner off a rangoon.

"Possible and true. And she used to eye me like she was going to put me on the curb for trash pickup when Mom wasn't looking."

"Why?" Brook asked, her eyes big with disbelief.

"Because she hated me," Uncle Wim said.

"Our mother didn't hate people!" Brook said.

Uncle Wim shrugged at Brook as if to say *You tell your story and I'll tell mine.*

"Why would she hate you?" Kobi asked. Their mother said it was wrong to hate people.

"Probably because my dad wasn't her dad, and Mom was the oldest mother on the planet when she had me. I was an embarrassment." He shrugged. "Plus, she was jealous. I was mighty cute." He grinned. After a while, he said, "I wish I'd gotten to know Bea better after we were grown up."

✶

That evening, in her pajamas, Kobi laid out her first-day-of-school clothes on the window seat. She loved the gray dress with the smocked top and the soft white collar. She loved it especially because the skirt flared and showed the pale pink lining when she twirled.

Brook came into the room, her toothbrush in her hand, to check for the third time that her shoes were perfectly lined up on the floor beneath her dress.

"Do you remember much about school?" Kobi asked.

Brook shook her head.

"Me neither."

Kobi was afraid she'd do something stupid because she didn't know any better. She was afraid kids would shy away from her because of her strange haircut.

Uncle Wim's footsteps came down the hall.

"You should be in bed, girls," he said. "It's nine o'clock. Big day tomorrow."

They said "Okay," but he kept standing in the doorway. Kobi hoped he wasn't going to kiss them good night like Grandmamma did. She blinked and shoved all thoughts of Grandmamma and Mr. Gyver and Madame Louise and the Paris apartment away.

Uncle Wim kept standing there. And Kobi and Brook kept standing there, too, as if they were playing statue and somebody had cried *"Freeze!"* Uncle Wim's gaze traveled around the room. When they landed on the school clothes on the window seat, his eyebrows jumped. Were they not allowed to lay things on the window seat?

His eyes moved to them. His expression looked very mixed up. He cleared his throat. "Well," he said. "Lights-out in fifteen minutes, okay?"

They nodded.

Fifteen minutes later, Kobi squirmed to get comfortable in bed. Her neck and ears felt exposed. She covered them up even though it was too hot.

Outside their windows, birds were bedding down, their cheeps trailing off to an occasional twitter. And then silence. Sleep came like a door swinging shut.

✳

She jerked upright, awakened by the carillon bonging midnight, and remembered where she was.

If it was midnight in Des Moines, it was seven a.m. in Paris, and Grandmamma would be in the dining room sipping coffee and nibbling a croissant. If Kobi were there, the petit point seat of the dining room chair would be velvety soft against her bare legs, and Grandmamma would remind Kobi to pull her hair back from her face.

Kobi lifted her face to the fan as it swept over her, making her scalp prickle. She ran her hand up the stubble on the back of her head.

She could not go to school like this. She had never needed to make hair grow really, really quickly. Plus, the magic usually wasn't effective when it was just for herself. But since her strange appearance embarrassed Brook and probably Uncle Wim . . .

Of the magic words Kobi hadn't yet figured out how to use, *frippery* felt the most likely. She sat on the edge of the bed, feet on the floor, hands on her knees, back very straight, and commanded her hair to grow. *Frippery.* She said it again, spreading out the syllables, trying to capture the magic of the word. *Fripp. Er. Ry.*

When she touched her head and there was nothing new, she cried. She tried all the other words she didn't know how to use. *Fiddlesticks, hogwash, carillon, buoy, parsimonious, lingua franca.*

Nothing. Not one eensy-weensy bit.

She would have to run away. In Paris, she would go to the park. On the far side was a lake, and at the edge of the lake was a willow tree. Under the branches, one day, she had discovered a private dome glowing with pale green light. Nobody would find her there.

But she was not in Paris, and the sun wasn't shining. And she didn't know what Uncle Wim would do if she ran away. The edges of her plan curled and turned to ash.

HOGWASH

EIGHT

*I*N the morning, she and Brook were ready at the door. Uncle Wim thudded overhead. Brook kept checking her backpack.

"Okay," Uncle Wim said, galloping down the stairs. "We're late. Let's go."

Despite looking like a freak in a beautiful dress, Kobi felt a *frisson* of excitement. She threw back her shoulders. Her parents would be proud of her courage.

When they were almost to Kobi's school and her stomach felt like she had swallowed a hopping toad, Uncle Wim said, "Sally will pick you up and keep you until I get off work. And I'm supposed to explain something. Her mother is ill."

"What's wrong with her?" Brook asked.

He swerved into a parking lot. "I don't have time to go into it all now." He grabbed a parking space and got out, whipping open Kobi's door. "Gotta hustle. Do you want to come along or stay here?" he asked Brook, who looked frozen.

"Stay here. I guess."

"Bye," Kobi said to Brook, her throat tight.

Brook opened her mouth to say something, but Uncle Wim slammed the door and put his hand on Kobi's shoulder. "Gotta hurry."

Kobi threw back her shoulders again and looked straight ahead as Uncle Wim steered her under the portico and through the double doors.

As they walked down the crowded hall, Uncle Wim said, "By tomorrow this will be old hat."

All around them, locker doors banged. A voice blared out of a loudspeaker, but Kobi couldn't understand a word the person was saying. Uncle Wim guided her into her classroom, where a teacher with frizzy hair and bright lipstick waited.

"Kobi Alighieri reporting for fifth grade," Uncle Wim said.

Charts and maps papered the walls. Carts of books filled the corners. Games and folders overflowed from the shelves beneath the windows. The carpet looked like a kaleidoscope.

Uncle Wim squeezed her shoulder. "See you tonight."

Dizzily, she nodded.

Ms. Carlson showed Kobi her locker and desk and where to sign up for hot lunch. Then she introduced Kobi to a pair of girls, one of whom held a white rabbit.

Kobi's hand went to her heart and she caught her breath. Had their precious lost Dante somehow found his way to Horace Mann School? She reached out to touch him.

"Don't!" the girl snapped, shaking her head and making her blond ponytail swish. "He doesn't know you. He knows me because my sister was in Ms. Carlson's classroom last year and she brought Peter home for the summer. And Peter knows Lily because we basically live at each other's houses."

"Anna and I are BFFs," Lily said.

"My mother is president of the PTO," Anna said. "Where did you go to school last year?"

Kobi knew as truly as her last name was Alighieri that she shouldn't reveal that this was her first day of school since kindergarten and she had no idea what they were talking about.

"Why are you dressed like that?" Lily asked. "Are you Amish?"

Kobi didn't know what Amish meant, so she probably wasn't. "I'm French."

"*French?*" they said.

She touched the gray dress. "This is how Parisians dress." It was certainly not how anybody else at Horace Mann Elementary dressed.

Lily stared at Kobi's patent leather sandals. Her gaze rose

over Kobi's dress and up to Kobi's hair. "You don't sound French," she finally said.

"Say something in French," Anna commanded.

"*J'aime les lapins*," Kobi said, aching to stroke the bunny's soft ears, to look under his left front paw for the little heart-shaped freckle. If he was Dante, would he remember her? She had grown, but that probably wouldn't matter to a bunny.

"Humph," Anna said, turning away.

Kobi stood by herself. She shouldn't have lied about being French. She hadn't really meant to. Grandmamma always quoted Sir Walter Scott. *Oh, what a tangled web we weave. When first we practise to deceive.* But Grandmamma shouldn't have dumped her in this crazy place.

Ms. Carlson whistled shrilly. How could one person teach so many kids? Kobi never thought she'd miss Mademoiselle, but she found herself blinking back tears.

Their desks were in small groups, facing each other. When Kobi sat down, she faced a boy with hair the color of a clementine. His large, pale blue eyes seemed to have been put on the wrong face.

"You've been in this room fourteen minutes and nine seconds and this is the first time you've noticed me," he said. "Care to guess why?"

Kobi shook her head.

"Do it anyway," he insisted.

"Because I've had lots of other things to look at?" Her

eyes kept going to the bunny cage. Was Dante looking at her?

"Because of my shirt," the boy said.

His shirt was brown and yellow.

He touched it. "These stripes are good for blending into an urban environment. And that's my goal for the year. To blend in."

Kobi wished she could blend in. Actually, she wished she could disappear.

"Was that your dad who brought you?" the boy asked.

"My uncle," she said. She would tell nothing but the truth from now on.

"Are your parents, the King and Queen, imprisoned by the evil sorcerer Krom? Did you shave off your hair to weave a shield of invisibility to escape and get help?" He didn't wait for her to answer. "Is that why you're living with your uncle?"

She was in a seating group with a crazy person.

He snapped his fingers. "Wait. I've *got* it! And *that*'s why you're wearing princess clothes!"

How could Grandmamma have been so wrong about appropriate school clothing?

"And if you need to disguise yourself as a boy, the hair is good." His eyes flashed. "That's my story, see? And I just put you in it. What's your name?"

Although she probably shouldn't have, she told him—even spelling *Alighieri*. She watched him write it down.

"Oh," he said, "and so you know. I never watch TV. If I see it accidentally, I turn my head. It rots the brain and retards healthy development in people under the age of twenty-two."

Kobi shut her eyes and took a deep breath.

★

At lunch in the cafeteria, which bounced everybody's voice around until it made Kobi's head throb, she was completely befuddled. She ended up at a table with a group of girls, including Anna and Lily.

"This is Kooky," Anna yelled, introducing her. "She's from *Paris*."

"Kobi," Kobi said above the din of clattering plastic trays. "Kobi Alighieri."

"That's what she said," Lily insisted. "Kooky. Kooky Ali-not-hairy."

The girls giggled and looked at each other.

Kobi blinked. Why were they being so mean? *Hogwash*, she muttered under her breath. It seemed like a good word for mean people. And it did make her feel better. *Hogwash!*

MALLEABLE

NINE

ᴬFTER school, she waited under the portico. What if Sally Hancock forgot to pick her up? What if Sally Hancock didn't know where the school was? What if Kobi didn't recognize Sally Hancock's car? Kobi stared anxiously at every car as it came to the head of the line in the pickup area.

Finally, *finally*, she saw Sally behind the wheel, smiling and waving.

Kobi scrambled into the backseat. She had survived one day.

A lady with short gray hair and dark eyes peered over the seat back at Kobi. She tilted her head to one side and then the other like a pigeon. "Sally, this child doesn't belong to us. Put her back before we get in *t-r-o-u-b-l-e*."

Kobi's eyes flew to Sally Hancock.

"Mom, this is Wim's niece. Remember, we talked about Kobi and Brook coming to visit? Kobi, this is my mother, Patricia Hancock."

"Hello," Kobi said, although she was confused.

Sally Hancock caught Kobi's eyes in the mirror. "That haircut shows off your face very prettily."

Something about Ms. Hancock's gaze gave Kobi the heebie-jeebies. "Beatrice," Ms. Hancock finally said, clearly speaking to Kobi, "how *is* your mother? I've not seen Amelia in ages."

Kobi swallowed. "I'm not Beatrice. I'm her daughter. Amelia is my grandmother."

Which made Kobi remember. She'd been so caught up in her own trials, she hadn't thought once about the wedding. Grandmamma and Mr. Gyver were married by now!

"Our grandmother got married today," she told Ms. Hancock. "Mr. Gyver is our stepgrandfather now."

"*Leonard* Gyver?"

Kobi nodded.

Ms. Hancock's scorching stare could have melted Kobi, leaving behind only bones, teeth, a new backpack, and the stupidest first-day-of-school dress ever.

Ms. Hancock sputtered. "You tell that trollop Amelia he's *my* husband. *Mine!*" She whipped around and stared straight ahead, making strange noises.

Kobi blinked. Grandmamma was what? Sally Hancock caught Kobi's eyes again. "Wim *did* explain about Mom's Alzheimer's, right?"

Kobi shook her head. She didn't know what that meant. But she was kind of figuring it out.

Brook's school was only a couple of blocks away. As they waited in the pickup line, Kobi saw her sister talking to a dark-haired girl. Had Brook made a friend already?

When Brook got into the car, Kobi wanted to fling her arms around her sister.

Sally Hancock said, "Mom, remember we talked about Kobi and Brook coming to visit Wim? This is Brook, the other sister. Brook, this is my mother, Patricia Hancock."

"Hello," Brook said. "I'm pleased to meet you."

Ms. Hancock smiled. "I'm pleased to meet you, too. I didn't know Wim had another sister."

Brook frowned.

"Dotty," Kobi mouthed silently.

Brook's eyes widened.

There was a lady in Grandmamma's apartment building who talked to invisible people in the elevator. Grandmamma called her *dotty*. Grandmamma said she certainly hoped *she* never became dotty.

Kobi spotted the Hancocks' house from down the block because of the pillar of chairs. They went through a side door into a cozy kitchen with a table in front of a window. Sally Hancock got out a carton of milk and a bag of cookies for Kobi and Brook. Then she took her mother upstairs to rest.

Kobi was ravenous. She took a bite of cookie, then a sip

of milk, letting the cold liquid soften the cookie inside her mouth.

"Why does your mother think we're Uncle Wim's sisters?" Brook asked when Sally came back.

"I think it's Kobi's haircut," she said. "It takes Mom back to an earlier time."

"Why does your mom think Mr. Gyver is her husband?" Brook asked.

"Because he was."

"Is Mr. Gyver your . . . *dad?*" Kobi asked. That would be very strange. It would make Sally Hancock their half stepaunt. Sort of.

"Oh no. I came along much later. But when they were young, Leonard Gyver and your grandfather were roommates. They married sorority sisters. Mom and Amelia were in each other's weddings. But Mom turned out not to be the marrying kind. Amelia took Leonard's side in the breakup. She said Mom broke Leonard's heart. So . . ." Sally Hancock shrugged.

So that was the reason Grandmamma didn't like the Hancocks. One mystery solved.

"Have you and Uncle Wim always known each other?" Kobi asked.

"We both grew up in the Bay Area. We met at camp when we were kids. Have you girls ever been to camp?"

"Grandmamma doesn't like camp. But we've gone fishing at Mr. Gyver's farm."

"It's probably best not to mention him when Mom is

around," Sally said. "Do you girls have homework?"

"Yes!" Brook said, beaming. "Tons!"

"How about you, Kobi?"

Kobi shook her head.

"Really?" Brook said, looking at her.

Truthfully, Kobi didn't know. The day had been that confusing.

Ms. Hancock called for her daughter, and Sally went upstairs.

When she was out of earshot, Brook said, "I love this house. I wish Uncle Wim's house was like this."

Kobi nodded. The house was small, but it was filled with bright pots and bowls, paintings and woven things. Purple and apricot and marigold colors covered the walls. There were books everywhere, a lot of them on gardening.

Brook unloaded her backpack and arranged her things on the table, pencils and pens in a row, their bottoms even with each other. "Sixth graders have daily planners." She opened a spiral notebook and showed Kobi a list. "This is what I have to do for tomorrow. I'll check things off when they're done, and Uncle Wim will initial the page." She closed the daily planner with a satisfied smile.

Kobi slid down in her chair until her chin was even with the table.

"You'll get bad posture if you sit like that," Brook said.

Who cared? But Kobi straightened up to get another cookie. "When you come to my school . . ." The look on

Brook's face stopped her. "You're coming, right?"

Brook dropped her eyes. "I kind of like my school

"Yesterday you cried because we couldn't be toget

"But my teacher is very nice," Brook said. "She plimented me profusely on my organizational skills I've made a friend already. Her name is Isabel. She lov clothes. And she's well organized, too."

"Then I'll go to your school," Kobi said. Isabel shou get ideas.

Brook glanced away.

"Is it my hair?" Tears stung Kobi's eyes. She couldn't it if she looked freaky. It was only until her hair grew.

"No."

"Then what?"

"Sixth grade is hard, Kobi. You have to be mature."

"But you can't leave me!"

They heard Sally Hancock's footsteps on the stairs.

"You're not quite ready for sixth grade," Brook said q etly, opening a book.

Kobi would talk to Grandmamma. Grandmamma wou *make* Brook go to Horace Mann Elementary. She woul make Brook be her best friend just as she had always beer *Malleable.*

✳

Before long, Uncle Wim's car turned into the drive. Sally said she'd be right back and slipped out the door. Although it wasn't polite, Kobi moved to where she could see them.

Uncle Wim leaned against the car door, pulled Sally Hancock into his arms, and gave her a long smooch. And Sally Hancock smooched Uncle Wim right back.

Kobi waved Brook over.

"Gross!" Brook clapped her hand over her eyes. "Do you think they're in love?" she asked, peeking between her fingers.

"They can't be. Grandmamma says Sally Hancock isn't Uncle Wim's type. Plus, Grandmamma says she's years older."

"She doesn't look older," Brook said. "I think they're in love."

Grandmamma was wrong about at least two things.

Kobi wondered what Sally and Uncle Wim were talking about as they stood in the shade beside Uncle Wim's car. He took money from his wallet and held it out to Sally.

She shook her head.

Uncle Wim tried to tuck the money into her shorts pocket. Sally pushed his hands away.

"What's he doing?" Brook asked. "Why is he giving her money?"

"Probably for helping with us."

"But he's unfortunate," Brook said.

Temporarily, Kobi said silently.

As Sally Hancock and Uncle Wim turned toward the house, Kobi and Brook scrambled into their chairs. *Temporarily,* Kobi said silently again, feeling guilty because they were costing Uncle Wim money.

PANTALOONS

TEN

*T*HE next morning, Kobi passed over the clothes Grand-mamma had bought her for school. She put on shorts and a sailor shirt as if she were going to play in the park. Even then, she didn't look like the other kids at Horace Mann.

When she got downstairs, Brook was in the kitchen wearing one of her Parisian dresses. Brook looked taller and older in Des Moines than she'd looked in Paris. They didn't look like a pair anymore. That was what the Great Alighieri called them. His Amazing Pair! His Best Magic Trick Ever! Kobi could feel his warm, proud gaze. She blinked away sudden tears.

Brook, her back to Kobi, was clattering around in the silverware drawer.

"What are you doing?" Kobi asked.

Brook jumped and slammed the drawer. "Nothing. And don't sneak around like that."

"I know what you're doing," Kobi said. "You're counting the silverware, making sure it divides evenly. If it doesn't, you're going to fly into a tizzy."

Brook stared.

Kobi knew she should shut up, but Brook was mean not to come to Kobi's school or let Kobi go to her school. "Does Isabel know you're weird?" she asked.

Brook bit her bottom lip. Looking straight ahead, she marched past Kobi and upstairs.

Kobi poured cereal into a bowl. She prickled with shame. Brook didn't bug her about the footlocker and Kobi didn't bug her about her *little rituals,* as Grandmamma called them. It was a sister rule.

When Uncle Wim came into the kitchen, he asked where Brook was.

Kobi watched her tasteless cereal float in the thin milk. "Upstairs, I guess."

"You girls aren't fighting, are you?"

When Kobi didn't answer, Uncle Wim put a finger under her chin and tilted her face up. "You mustn't," he said, "because I've got all I can handle in the morning."

His eyebrows had a tiny little curve upward at the ends. When she looked at Uncle Wim, she saw both Grandmamma and her mother.

"May I call Grandmamma?" she asked.

Uncle Wim handed her the phone. "If you happen to mention Sally's mother, skip the part about the Alzheimer's, okay?"

Kobi had a long list of things she couldn't talk to Grandmamma about. She didn't want to say anything about staying at the Hancocks' because Grandmamma had gotten mad that they were going there after school. She'd overheard Uncle Wim on the phone Sunday afternoon saying Grandmamma was going to have to trust him to make good decisions. Yes, he could have made different arrangements for after-school care, but not better ones. He was not fourteen anymore. Kobi couldn't talk about Sally because Grandmamma wouldn't want to hear that Uncle Wim and Sally were in love. She couldn't talk about Ms. Hancock because the most important thing about her was something Kobi wasn't allowed to tell. She couldn't talk about herself because she didn't want Grandmamma to know about the haircut and the clothes. And she couldn't talk about changing schools because if Brook didn't want to be with Kobi, Kobi didn't want to be with Brook.

Kobi handed the phone back to Uncle Wim. "Maybe later," she said. "But why can't I tell her about Ms. Hancock's illness?"

Uncle Wim unwrapped a granola bar. "If Patricia were herself, she wouldn't want Mom to know. So Sally doesn't want Mom to know, either."

"Why not?"

Uncle Wim sighed. "Mom and Patricia were always competitors. They would *never* show each other their weaknesses."

Uncle Wim went to the foot of the stairs and called up. "Brook! Blastoff in five minutes."

"Grandmamma thinks you and Sally Hancock are just friends because Sally is so much older than you."

Uncle Wim's face turned red. "Only three years," he finally said. "Okay. More like four."

When Brook came downstairs, she didn't look at Kobi. Uncle Wim handed her a granola bar.

On the way to school, the space between them felt like a great stone wall. The granola bar stayed unopened in Brook's hand.

As they were turning into the drop-off area, Kobi touched Brook's hand. Brook's eyes met hers. "*Pantaloons*," Kobi whispered, and crossed her eyes. It was the only magic word she said out loud to anyone. It was a sister word. Brook tried not to smile. Her lips quivered and she finally gave up. She laughed. Kobi smiled.

When she got to her classroom, girls playing a card game at the reading table said she could join in, but Kobi shook her head. She'd heard Ms. Carlson tell them to invite her.

She sat at her desk and pretended to look at the book on islands she'd checked out during library time the day before. Dante was in his cage and nobody else was paying any attention to him. She could pick him up and look at his paw, find the heart-shaped freckle and know for sure. But she didn't. The orange-haired boy in a two-toned green striped shirt stood in front of a rain forest poster.

After the bell, Ms. Carlson told them to get out their math worksheets. The orange-haired boy, whose name was Norman, and another boy, whose name was Alejandro, got out worksheets with lots of writing on them.

Did she have a worksheet?

Ms. Carlson walked around the room, glancing at their papers. She didn't say anything when she passed Kobi's naked desk, but Kobi felt her notice. Kobi's bare ears and neck flamed.

During morning recess, a girl asked Kobi with a smirk if Kobi's outfit was from Paris.

"Yes," Kobi admitted. All her clothes were.

The girl nodded and went off to join other girls, and they kept sneaking peeks at Kobi.

The playground lady informed Kobi that it wasn't allowed to just stand in the shade during recess. Even Norman, who would have blended in perfectly in the shade, was running around playing something.

"But I don't know how to play those games. And I don't have on play shoes."

"Because Kooky is from *Paris*," Lily sang as she ran past. *Hogwash!*

The playground lady put her hand on Kobi's shoulder and steered her into a game of foursquare, and Kobi felt very stupid as the kids explained the rules. One of the girls said, "Where did you go to school last year?"

When the bell finally rang, they lined up at the door to go in. Kobi didn't understand why they had to line up for everything. In the line, she heard the word *stuck-up*.

She was the first person back to the classroom, and Ms. Carlson spoke to her quietly about math worksheets. She said Kobi should do one every night. They would help build her skills. Although she was nice, Ms. Carlson probably thought Kobi was stupid.

During silent reading time, Kobi opened a book and practically threw herself onto the island. *Avanti!* she breathed silently.

In the tree house, a breeze stirred the leaves. Her mother was weaving a mat out of soft grass. The fronds made a shushing sound as they passed between her mother's fingers. Sometimes her mother hummed part of a song. She was wearing the soft sun-faded blue shirt. Kobi buried her face in the shirt. But her mother kept on weaving, her body moving back and forth as if Kobi weren't even there. After all this time, it still broke Kobi's heart that her mother didn't see her. Looking down through the branches, she watched her dad drag a net out of the sea. Even from so high up, she could see the wriggling fish, their bodies silvery in the sunlight. She wanted to scream *Fix the boat!* but she knew he wouldn't hear her.

★

Kobi nearly leapt out of her chair when the bell rang. Bells and lines. She hated them.

After science, she lined up to go to the cafeteria, and after lunch she lined up to go onto the playground. And because she wasn't allowed to stand in the shade, she played kickball even though she had on sandals. And because one of the sandals broke when she kicked the ball, she fell and skidded across the asphalt.

"Are you okay?" the playground lady asked, bending over her.

Kobi couldn't find her voice. Her knees felt as if they'd been ripped off.

She sat up and looked at her scraped knees. They were grayish white. She looked at her hands. They were the same strange color. And then they began to ooze blood. Then the trees began to spin. The monkey bars melted. The playground lady's face was a fun-house face.

"You need to see the nurse," the playground lady said, helping Kobi up.

She felt a fat trickle of blood run down her leg. The broken sandal flapped when she walked. She was bathed in cold sweat. She would not cry.

Ms. Johnson, the nurse, had beautiful wavy hair like Kobi's mother. She left a message for Uncle Wim about Kobi's accident. She took off the broken sandal, pronounced it history, and began to clean the scrapes, spraying them with something that didn't sting. One cut on Kobi's knee required a butterfly bandage. The nurse was putting it on when Uncle Wim called back.

After Ms. Johnson talked to him, she held out the phone. "Your uncle would like to speak with you."

Was he going to yell at her the way he had when she'd used the stove? But none of this was Kobi's fault. She wouldn't have worn sandals if she'd known she had to play running games.

"I remember those skids across the playground," Uncle Wim said. "They pretty much rip your skin off." His voice was warm, like a puppy licking her. "Does it hurt a lot?"

She couldn't help it. She burst into heaving sobs. And the sobs turned into wails. "I want to go home! I want to go back to Paris!"

The nurse was kind. She visited with Kobi about Paris, and then she played Scrabble with Kobi until school was over. And the dismissal bell was the best sound Kobi had ever heard.

As she waited in the pickup area, wearing a pair of thick gym socks that Ms. Johnson had in her drawer, the boy in the striped shirt wandered over.

"I have something," he said out of the side of his mouth, staring at the shrubbery.

Kobi looked around. "Are you talking to me?"

"Yes. You did battle with the forces of evil. You are bloody but not broken."

That was a good description of her second day at Horace Mann Elementary.

"Here's a beetle for you." He parted the folds of a piece of used spiral notebook paper. The beetle was about half an inch long and glistened like sea glass. "See the iridescence?" he said.

That was one of her most amazing magic words! She looked into his pale eyes to see if there was some secret message in them, but he blushed and looked away.

Kobi watched the beetle's legs churn, but it couldn't go anywhere because it was deep in the fold of the paper. "It's beautiful," she said.

He closed the paper gently and gave it to her. "I wrote the story it's wrapped in. You can keep the story, but you should let the beetle go." He nodded at her, making kind of a little bow, and then hurried to get into a car. The rims of his ears were as red as a sunset.

He was brave to talk to her and give her a present when she looked as if she'd been partially eaten by a bear and everyone thought she was stuck-up.

✸

"Whoa!" Brook cried, getting into the car. "What happened to you?"

"I fell playing kickball," Kobi said.

She could feel the beetle churning in the paper. He seemed to be slowing down. *Dimpling,* she said silently, hoping that would keep him alive until she could let him out in a good place.

The minute they pulled into the Hancocks' drive, Kobi got out and knelt in the grass even though it hurt her skinned knees.

"What are you doing?" Brook asked, squatting beside her.

Kobi opened the paper. The glistening beetle walked to the edge, went over it, walked on the underside of the paper, and then disappeared into the shadows.

"Well, that was weird," Brook said. "Why were you carrying around a bug?"

"A boy gave it to me."

"Do you have a *boy*friend?"

"No! He's just a boy." She told Brook about Norman's quirks and funny attempts to blend in.

When she was finished, Brook pursed her lips. "We're new girls and who we make friends with is important so we get off on the right foot. Isabel explained it. So maybe you don't want someone like Norman for a friend. He sounds odd."

"Oh, pish! Isabel," Kobi said. Then she stopped. She had been mean about Isabel this morning. So she zipped her lips and followed Brook inside.

Sally Hancock put out milk and cookies, and this time Ms. Hancock joined them. When the marigolds on the table made Kobi sneeze, Ms. Hancock said, *"Gesundheit! Sleep tight!"*

It was hard not to laugh—especially when Brook caught her eye. "Thank you," Kobi said.

After the snack, she puzzled over her math worksheet. She asked Brook for help, but Brook said she didn't have time to do her own work and Kobi's, too. Kobi couldn't ask Sally for help because she and Ms. Hancock had gone out to tie up tomatoes. Kobi had an image of tomatoes straining at their knots, trying to break loose and run free in the neighborhood. She drew that on the back of her math worksheet; then she turned the sheet over and wrote any old thing between the questions and hoped Ms. Carlson didn't look closely.

It was already dusk when Uncle Wim called to tell Sally Hancock he would be there in half an hour. She told him she'd make macaroni and cheese.

Kobi's mouth watered. She *loved* Madame Louise's macaroni and cheese casserole, which filled the whole apartment with the aroma of baking cream and cheese. But Sally Hancock's macaroni and cheese rattled out of a box into a pan of boiling water and was served up in ten minutes. It was a funny shade of runny yellow. It was not real food, but Kobi was hungry. *Scrambled,* she said silently, and it was good.

Later, while Brook was running her bedtime bath in the tub, which Uncle Wim now called the Fastest Filler in the West, Kobi sat in the star-papered little room, which they'd christened their closet. She sat on the floor, leaning against the footlocker. A window, open a crack, ruffled her pajamas. The air that blew on her was the same air that blew on her parents. It was almost like being hugged by them.

The faint sounds of Uncle Wim's baseball game came through the floor. When Brook turned off the water, pipes clanged.

Earlier, Kobi had heard Uncle Wim ask Brook what was in the footlocker. Brook didn't know. Nobody did. They were things that would be needed when her parents got home. She turned and pressed her cheek against the hasp.

After a while, she turned on the clever little flashlight Mr. Gyver had given her for Christmas, the one shaped like a credit card with a Monet painting on one side and a Pissarro painting on the other. She shone it on the paper Norman had wrapped the beetle in.

Krom was an evil pirate and a sorcerer too. His terrible weakness was that he required a constant supply of pairs to keep his powers from waning. Pairs of anything. So Krom and his minions hunted the seas, shanghaiing hapless ships and stealing all the pairs they could find. Dice. Twins. Gloves. Bookends. Shoes. Earrings. Eyeglasses. Socks. Trousers. Earmuffs. Parents.

The twins and the parents were the hardest to steal because they put up a fight. But when he said the Be-Still Words to them, they folded like pieces of warm pizza.

When he had a good catch, Krom set sail for

the hidden cove on the coast of Meanderhieden. When he came to the white cliffs, the pirate king tacked windward to his castle.

Once his human catch was dumped like fish in the dungeons, their only hope lay in the small colony of beetles that lived in the roots of the milkweed plant growing along the edge of the moat. These enchanted, magical beetles shone with iridescence. Their mission was to carry messages between the prisoners and people in the world who loved and missed them.

So anytime you see one of these iridescent beetles, and you can see them often if you look in the right places, remember two things. 1) Pirates are real and very dangerous. 2) People in our hearts are real, too.

Kobi's hand went to her heart. Why did the story make her sad? Make her think of her parents? They weren't in a dungeon. Pirates didn't have them.

But she said *Avanti!* to be sure.

And there they were. The beach fire crackled, sending fireflies into the darkness. The wind was blowing, the trees at the edge of the forest swaying. Her parents sat in the sand, her mom's head on her dad's shoulder. They looked sad. They weren't saying anything, but Kobi knew they were missing home, missing her and Brook. Her dad stood up. He took her mother's hand. "Come on," he said, helping her to her feet. "Tomorrow is a whole new day."

FREESIA

ELEVEN

*T*HE days were the same. Get up and put on stupid Parisian clothes. Go to school and stick out like a sore thumb, as Madame Louise would say. Go to the Hancocks'. Get up and put on stupid Parisian clothes. Go to school . . .

Kobi couldn't ask Uncle Wim to buy her normal clothes because he was unfortunate. And Grandmamma would never understand because Grandmamma had a very sure fashion sense. Plus, she would logically wonder why the stylish dresses worked for Brook but not for Kobi. And Kobi couldn't explain what had happened between her and Brook. It was like lurching along with one shoe off and one shoe on.

On Tuesday of the third week, when she and Brook were in the kitchen helping Sally dry herbs from the garden,

Brook asked, "Why don't you buy parsley like Madame Louise does?"

"Does Madame Louise have any choice? Does your grandmother have room for a garden in her apartment?"

Brook shook her head.

"And this is grown organically not fifty feet away from where you're standing," Sally said. "It hasn't been shipped all around the world. Think of what that saves."

"But I saw worms on it in the garden," Brook said.

"Caterpillars," Kobi said.

Brook shrugged.

"Caterpillars will become butterflies," Kobi said. Sally told her if nothing ate the caterpillars on the parsley, they would become swallowtails. "And caterpillars have legs. Worms don't," Kobi said. She had drawn a picture of the green-and-black caterpillars on the parsley.

Ms. Hancock put on a paint-streaked smock. She arranged bottles of paint on the table. She laid out brushes and sponges, cotton swabs and fat pencils, two cups of water and a tiny vial of gold.

"What's she doing?" Brook asked as she tweaked parsley leaves into tidy columns and rows to make a perfect square on a paper towel.

"I don't know," Kobi said. She was arranging the leaves like a flock of swooping birds.

The herby smell made Kobi ache for Madame Louise's kitchen. It was eleven o'clock in Paris at that moment. Grandmamma might be in the kitchen having a cup of bedtime tea. She had decided not to accompany Mr. Gyver to Beijing to claim his prize because she was tired. She would rest until he got home, and then they would make their wedding trip.

"Why do you have so many books on gardening?" Brook asked.

Sally smiled. "Ask Wim."

"Beatrice," Ms. Hancock called, motioning to Kobi to come to her.

Kobi looked at Sally.

"It's okay," she told Kobi.

Kobi would rather have finished the flight path of her parsley birds, but she crossed the kitchen and sat in the chair Ms. Hancock gestured to.

"May I have your arm?" Ms. Hancock asked.

Kobi glanced at Sally again. Sally smiled.

When Kobi stretched her arm out on the table, Ms. Hancock turned it so Kobi's palm was up. She ran her fingers over Kobi's skin as if she were inspecting a melon at the grocer's.

She dipped a brush into red paint. With a few tickly strokes, she made five petals on Kobi's arm. Then she dipped into the yellow paint and swirled the brush over the petals, and a lovely orange blossom appeared, showing a bit of yellow in places and a deep, dark red at the heart. Ms. Hancock blew on the flower, and Kobi shivered at the prickle of drying paint.

Ms. Hancock chose a fat pencil with a soft, crayon-like tip and outlined part of the petals. Then she patted a tiny sponge filled with purple paint around the blossom and began to send vines of leaves and flowers twining up Kobi's arm. Kobi sat perfectly still.

It took a very long time. Insects and butterflies—even a swallowtail caterpillar—came out of the shadows to feed on the flowers. A beetle like the one Norman had given her crawled on a leaf. Ms. Hancock used a streak of paint from the gold vial to highlight his shell. Her touch made Kobi remember her mother brushing and braiding Kobi's hair when Kobi was little—Grandmamma rubbing sunscreen on Kobi's shoulders at the beach. *Freesia,* Kobi said silently, gazing at the top of Ms. Hancock's head as she bent over Kobi's arm.

Kobi relaxed so deeply her toes went limp and she felt like purring. *Freesia.* It was the first time she had felt that way in Des Moines. She was sorry when Ms. Hancock was finished.

"It's beautiful," Kobi said.

Ms. Hancock looked exhausted but also happy.

"It's absolutely lovely, Mom," Sally said.

"One of my smaller installations," Ms. Hancock said.

And Uncle Wim, when he got there, praised the arm extravagantly. Only Brook ignored Kobi's fabulous arm and turned her nose up so high she could have drowned in the rain.

On the way to Uncle Wim's house, Brook asked Uncle Wim why he and Sally had so many books on gardens, chickens, and stuff like that.

He met their eyes in the mirror. "We'd like to start a communal organic garden someday."

"Why?" Kobi asked.

"It seems like a good thing to do," he said. "But don't get me started. It's in the future. Sally has her hands full. So do I."

Kobi snuck a look at Brook. Because Grandmamma had dropped them here.

That night, Kobi took a one-armed bath so the paint wouldn't wash off. She slept with her arm hanging off the bed so the paint wouldn't smear. She wore a sleeveless shirt to school so the amazing arm wouldn't be hidden.

"You're going to get made fun of," Brook said.

Kobi shrugged. Brook didn't know Kobi got made fun of all the time.

"Don't say I didn't warn you."

In Ms. Carlson's room, Anna and Lily were hogging the bunny as always. And because Kobi's desk was near his cage, Anna was the first to notice Kobi's arm.

"What *happened*?"

Lily gawked. "Is that a *tattoo*?"

"No!" Grandmamma would never allow tattoos.

A couple of other kids wandered over to look.

"It's body painting." Kobi moved her arm, making the insects stir.

"It's alive!" a boy cried.

"Why would you want *that* on your body?" somebody asked.

"It's creepy," a girl said.

"It's art," Kobi said.

Anna took a closer look. "Art?"

"It was painted by a famous artist." The kids needed to appreciate Ms. Hancock's beautiful work.

"What's this famous artist's name?" Lily asked.

Kobi gave Ms. Hancock's name the weight of Amelia Earhart or Mother Teresa when she said, "Patricia Hancock."

Everybody just looked at her, so she said it again. "Patricia *Hancock*?" She widened her eyes with a surely-you've-heard-of-*her* gesture.

After a beat, a boy snorted, "I thought you were going to say *Picasso*!" and nearly turned himself inside out laughing.

Anna looked skeptical. Kobi rushed on. "Patricia Hancock is known all over the world for creating things that are beautiful but don't last. Like this." Like the chairs in the yard, which had fallen down while they were eating dinner the night before. Kobi would have to wash off the art tonight because Sally said it could hurt her skin if she kept it on longer. "Patricia Hancock is a friend of my grandmother's in Paris."

That was such a huge lie, Kobi was surprised the floor didn't open and swallow her.

But Anna was looking a tiny bit impressed.

Lily said, "If she's a friend of your grandmother's in Paris, how did she paint your arm in Des Moines?"

"She's visiting her daughter, who is my uncle's friend." Kobi's heart was pounding. *Oh, what a tangled web we weave* . . .

"Really?" Anna said.

Kobi nodded. She felt her story start to collapse under the weight of their silence.

"That's awesome," Anna said.

Kobi let out her breath slowly.

Anna turned to Lily. "Your mother should invite the famous artist to paint bodies for your birthday party. It would make the party more interesting." She smiled at Kobi. "And you could come."

Lily scowled. "We don't have room for more guests. And my mother already has the event planned."

Anna shrugged. "It's your party."

Ms. Carlson told them to take their seats.

Norman wasn't in school that morning. Kobi hoped he got to see her beautiful vine before she washed it off. She felt so heady from her victory with Anna that she didn't hear a word Ms. Carlson was saying. She was dizzy with relief that she hadn't gotten caught in the lies, but she promised herself she would never *ever* lie again. Not the teeniest tiniest lie. She'd rather go without friends than have to worry about getting caught every second.

During computer time, Lily asked if they could go online and research the famous artist Patricia Hancock. Her voice sounded innocent, but the smile she gave Kobi was evil.

Kobi stopped breathing. She was going to get caught after all. Ms. Carlson would tell Uncle Wim she was a liar, and Uncle Wim would tell Grandmamma and Brook and Sally, and Grandmamma would tell Mr. Gyver and Madame Louise.

"Shall we do that, Kobi?" Ms. Carlson asked.

"Sure," Kobi said, knowing there was no way out.

Anna and Lily and a few others gathered around Ms. Carlson as she put in her password. Kobi knew better than to try a magic word. And she was glad Norman wasn't in school after all.

Ms. Carlson clicked away on the keyboard. She looked around. "Kobi, you should be over here, too."

Mortification buzzed in Kobi's head as she went to stand with the group.

Ms. Carlson clicked and scrolled. "Ah!" she said. "Here we are."

The woman in the picture was young, with flaming red hair. She wore a tank top and bell-bottoms.

Who was that?

The woman stood beside what looked like a giant mud castle that had been hit by a wave. The Golden Gate Bridge, partly shrouded in fog, loomed in the background.

Ms. Carlson read aloud. "'Patricia Hancock, born in 1946 in Monterey, California, studied at the Wilson School of Design.'"

Kobi leaned closer. That was *Ms. Hancock*?

Ms. Carlson kept reading. "'. . . a protégée of Manuel

Rivera . . . drew the greatest notice for her series of installations in the western United States and Central America . . .'"

As Ms. Carlson brought up more pictures of Ms. Hancock's installations around the world, Kobi caught Lily's eyes. Lily looked away.

Kobi touched her colorful arm. She really *had* been painted by the famous artist Patricia Hancock!

TEMPORARILY

TWELVE

*K*OBI was full of the news when she got into the car. Ms. Hancock had her picture in newspapers and magazines and even Wikipedia. If Ms. Hancock knew what Kobi was talking about, she gave no sign. She looked tired.

But Sally kept smiling at her mother. "Back in the day, Mom was an event."

When Brook got into the car she didn't believe Kobi until Sally said it was true. "The beautiful things in our house—the weaving, the pottery, the paintings—most of them are Mom's work. But her true passion is transient art. Things that don't last long."

"Does Uncle Wim know this?" Brook asked.

Sally laughed. "Of course. Remember, we grew up to-gether in the Bay Area."

"Does Grandmamma know?" Brook asked.

"Yes," Sally said.

Kobi remembered what Uncle Wim had said about Grandmamma and Ms. Hancock being competitors.

"Was Grandmamma famous, too?" Wouldn't that be something, if she had a famous grandmother and didn't even know it!

Sally hesitated. Finally, she said, "In a way."

"In what way?" Kobi pressed.

Sally waggled her hand as if to say *Oh, a little bit this way and a little bit that way.*

"Really, Sally, what is Grandmamma famous for?"

Sally brushed her hair behind her ear and asked Kobi if she'd like to deadhead marigolds. Kobi had no idea what that was, but clearly Sally wasn't going to answer her question.

✱

The shriveled-up blossoms made a satisfying *pop* when Kobi yanked them off the plants. They left her hands smelling spicy. Sally was on her hands and knees, feeling around in the dirt for sweet potatoes. A UPS truck turned into the drive, and a delivery guy dropped a package on the steps and waved to Kobi and Sally.

Sally wiped her hands on her jeans, found her phone, and called Uncle Wim. "They're here!" she said. She listened, smiling, then said, "Okay."

"Who's here?" Kobi asked.

"The red wigglers."

Kobi had no idea what Sally was talking about.

"You'll see." Sally laughed and shook her head. "Wim's coming home."

When he arrived, he and Sally carefully opened the package.

"May I see?" Kobi asked.

They made room for her. Uncle Wim said, "There are supposed to be five hundred. Does it look like five hundred to you?"

In a damp cardboard box a tangle of skinny, reddish worms with fine lines around their bodies writhed in brown stuff.

"Is that dirt?" Kobi asked.

"Castings," Uncle Wim said.

"Worm poo," Sally explained.

"Eww."

Uncle Wim said, "They're probably hungry."

Sally nodded. "I don't see any food particles left."

She went to the shed and returned with plastic bins. She lined the bottoms with cabbage leaves, carrot tops, the marigold blossoms Kobi had pulled off, and other bits of garden refuse.

"Okay," she said. "Ready for the wigglers. Want to help, Kobi?"

"Do we dump them in?"

"No," Uncle Wim said. "We need to separate them from the castings; then we'll make tea out of the castings."

Kobi put her hands over her mouth and Uncle Wim laughed.

"People don't drink it," he said. "After it's aerated and steeped, Sally will pour it around plants. Nutritional dynamite!"

Kobi saw Brook watching out the window. Kobi motioned to her, but Brook shook her head.

Kobi thought the brown stuff might stink, but it didn't really. It smelled kind of like the earth. "They don't bite or sting, do they?" she asked.

"Nope," Uncle Wim said, picking up a handful.

Eventually, they had five bins full of worms burrowing into the refuse.

"The food goes in one end and castings come out the other end," Uncle Wim said. "Except that what comes out is even better than what goes in because the worms clean out contaminants as they digest the food. It's called vermiculture. Imagine that!"

Uncle Wim sound as excited about vermiculture as Grandmamma sounded about museums and the ballet.

"Wow!" Kobi said.

★

After they'd feasted on fried zucchini—organic and very, *very* local, Sally pointed out—and soup from a can that would have made Madame Louise cringe but was okay under the charm of *scrambled,* and after they'd gone back to Uncle Wim's house, Brook announced she needed a desk.

"I need to keep my schoolwork organized. Isabel has a desk."

"You're only going to be here until Christmas," Uncle Wim said.

"I don't have my own room and Kobi moves my stuff."

They had always shared a room. They used to share a *bed*. "I don't know what's wrong with you," Kobi grumbled.

Brook's eyebrows rose. "I'm becoming more mature."

"And selfish!"

"Girls," Uncle Wim said tiredly. "Cut it out. Long day here. Brook, you can have a desk. You too, Kobi."

If Uncle Wim couldn't afford a big bed, he couldn't afford two desks. *Temporarily.* "I'll share Brook's," she said.

"You will *not*," Brook said. "That's the whole point."

"I don't need a desk," Kobi said. "I don't have homework."

"And why is that?" Brook asked. She looked at Uncle Wim. "I think fifth graders have homework."

"Well, I have *some*," Kobi admitted. "Like the interview assignment. But I don't need a desk."

She had interviewed Sally and made careful notes, dividing her report into the categories Ms. Carlson had given them: childhood, young adulthood, adulthood, later years. Sally hadn't had later years yet, but the other parts had been interesting. Sally had been an only child with two artist parents until there was only one artist parent—Ms. Hancock—because the other artist parent drifted off. When asked about her greatest adventure of young adulthood, Sally said it was almost being eaten by a bear in the High Sierras, where she was a junior counselor all summer, every summer. Then she changed her mind and said it wasn't the bear, it was Uncle Wim, who had kissed her one starry night, which was against the rules because he was a camper and she was a junior counselor. She hadn't been able to get rid of him since, Sally said, smiling at Uncle Wim when she told the story. She had gone to college at Santa Clara and waited for Uncle Wim to grow up. And she was still waiting. Uncle Wim had asked Kobi when she was going to interview *him*.

Kobi liked that kind of homework, and did a terrific report that Ms. Carlson praised, especially for the marginal illustrations.

Uncle Wim was looking at Kobi, his eyebrows going on a whole journey of their own. "Kobi, you're not forgetting about some of your homework, are you?"

"I have an excellent memory," she said. That was not a lie.

"Well, I think you'd both better have desks."

"But you can't afford two desks," Kobi said. If he could afford desks, why didn't he have dining room furniture or comfortable chairs for the living room?

"If something really needs to be done," Uncle Wim said, "there's usually a way to do it."

"Grandmamma could buy our desks," Kobi said. After all, it was Grandmamma who'd left them here.

"I don't need Mom's help," Uncle Wim said coolly.

"Did the worms cost a lot?" Kobi asked.

Uncle Wim's eyebrows twitched and he shook his head.

"Is Grandmamma famous?" Brook asked.

Uncle Wim looked perplexed.

"Sally said Grandmamma was famous in a way," Kobi said.

Uncle Wim sighed. "Time for you girls to take your baths and get to bed. Morning comes early."

Awhile later, as Kobi settled into warm water up to her chin, she watched the beautiful vine and beetles and butterflies vanish. The water turned a murky green and left a ring. She had to scrub with soap to get the outlines of some of the flowers and insects off her skin.

She felt sad, washing away Ms. Hancock's lovely work, but Sally said Ms. Hancock would want her to. To be alive was to change, Ms. Hancock taught her students. And to create art that lasted only a little while reminded people to eat soup while it was hot.

Kobi kind of got it. Everything *was* changing. She hadn't seen Grandmamma for almost a month. She no longer expected to glance up and see Mademoiselle. Brook was turning into a different person. Kobi was expected to make friends and do math worksheets.

And she was becoming an awful liar.

DILETTANTE

THIRTEEN

*T*HE next morning, rain came out of the sky as if a giant bucket were being dumped on the neighborhood. The wipers whipped from side to side. Uncle Wim said this was good, because central Iowa needed rain. But they were delayed because a traffic light was out. When Uncle Wim pulled under the overhang of Horace Mann Elementary, the silence boomed.

The first bell had rung, so Kobi hurried to her locker, then into the classroom and to her desk. The room was already quiet. Instead of walking around looking at math worksheets laid out on desks, Ms. Carlson was saying to fold them once vertically, then write their names and the date at the top and pass them to the front of the room. The worksheets would go in each student's folder for the upcoming parent-teacher conferences.

"Why?" Kobi whispered to Alejandro.

He shrugged. "What she said yesterday," he whispered.

Yesterday Kobi had been thinking about her painted arm during math.

She got out her worksheet. At a glance, it looked normal. Columns of numbers in straight rows with lines under them, plus signs, minus signs, times signs (she especially liked the X and used it a lot), equals signs, and then a label for whatever thing was being talked about in the word problem. Last night there had been a word problem about vegetables. Tomatoes, eggplants, and peppers were being planted in rows. She'd gone to the garden and used Sally's plants as models. She'd drawn pictures on the back of the worksheet. The glossy eggplants were an amazing shade of purple. She had thought about coloring her drawing, but decided that was babyish.

She thought her worksheet looked nice. But was Ms. Carlson really going to *read* it? What would Uncle Wim say when he saw drawings of eggplants on her math worksheet? She didn't want him to know she was a poor student. It would make him feel bad. She riffled through the magic words that so far had no uses.

As the lights dimmed for a long, slow minute and booming thunder made Kobi jump, the word that was left bouncing around in her head as the lights came back was *dilettante*.

She saw the way to protect Uncle Wim from knowing something that would make him sad. The conference was for parents. Uncle Wim wasn't her parent, so she wouldn't tell him. Problem solved.

It was still raining at morning recess, so they stayed in. Norman sat at his desk writing. He kept his stories in a ring binder that he didn't allow anybody to touch.

Kobi decided to draw a picture of Norman. He could put it on his ring binder like the author photo on the dust jacket of her mother's books. She asked him if it would be okay if she drew him.

"Sure. Make my shirt striped," he said. Today his T-shirt was navy and gray, the perfect rainy-day colors.

Kobi liked the rain. It was cozy and nobody was making her play stupid games or stand in line. Dante was in his cage, gazing at her, making her remember San Francisco. Norman bent over his work.

"My mother is a writer," Kobi told him.

"Oh yeah?" Norman said, looking up. "A famous writer?"

"No."

"Does she write fiction or nonfiction?"

"She creates characters," Kobi said, "and makes them do exactly what she wants them to."

"Yes!" Norman said, pumping his fist in the air. "Made-up things are way better than real things. So does your grandmother live with you?"

Why would he think that? "My grandmother lives in Paris."

"Then who's the older lady in the car with your mom every day?"

"Oh! That's not my mom. That's my uncle's girlfriend. And Ms. Hancock is *her* mom."

Norman cocked his head. "Hancock as in the famous artist? You get to ride in the same car with the famous artist every day?" His voice rose.

Kobi nodded, smiling. Norman was weird, but she liked him.

"You are so lucky!" he said.

She really was. Sometimes another person flashed out of Ms. Hancock's gray eyes. Somebody interesting and fun and very smart who Kobi wished could come out. Ms. Hancock was like a beautiful picture that had been rained on, then driven over by a car, then left under a pile of leaves to be nibbled by squirrels, and the only beautiful bit left was a tiny patch of incredible blue in one corner.

Last night, Kobi had started using the word *ragout* to make Ms. Hancock get well. But it was like *temporarily*—a person had to be patient to know for sure. Kobi and Brook had been helping Sally follow a recipe called Eight-Vegetable Ragout. When Brook asked what rag-out was, Sally corrected her, saying it was rah-*goo*. Kobi had been saying the word her mother gave her wrong all these years. No wonder it hadn't worked! She said *ragout* to herself the right way and Ms. Hancock stood, walked briskly to the door, got mail out of the mailbox, laid it on the counter, and sat back down in her chair. Sally had looked so surprised.

"So why does your uncle bring you to school and his girlfriend pick you up?" Norman asked. "What happened to your parents?"

"Nothing happened to them!" Kobi's heart leapt into her throat, and she was being too loud. Ms. Carlson was looking at her. "They're on a sailing trip, that's all," Kobi said quietly.

"To where?"

"The South Sea Islands."

"Really?" Norman looked overloaded with amazement. Kobi nodded.

"When will they be back?"

"I don't know. It could be tomorrow or it could be longer."

"Don't they tell you?"

"They can't always stay in touch." It was nice to talk about her parents with somebody who didn't give her funny looks. It was like kicking off shoes that were too tight. "Sometimes they're in places where they can't get a satellite signal. Sometimes they're about ready to start for home, and then something happens and they have a new adventure."

"Wow!" He let out a big breath. "My parents raise organic goats."

"There are goats on the island where my parents are now. My parents milk them." She told him about the wild pig that her dad had speared with a handmade weapon.

Norman gazed at her.

She told him how her parents wove a net from sea grass and used it to haul fish out of the surf. She told him about the steps that wound around the gnarled tree to the rooms where her parents lived. She told him how the rooms swayed ever so gently in the wind. She told him about the floor mats her mother made from grass.

"Man, it's like you've been there," Norman said. "The way you describe it!"

She wished she could tell him she'd been there many times. But not even Abnormal Norman, as the kids called him, would understand that.

"You must be really proud," he said. "They should make a *National Geographic* special about your parents."

"They're going to," she said, smiling, feeling so warm and happy the lie slipped out.

Norman gazed at her as if she were a rock star.

She hadn't meant to lie. She could explain that to Norman. She wanted to explain.

"Way better than organic goats," he said, shaking his head. "Way better."

★

At lunch, Anna put down her tray beside Kobi's. Norman was on Kobi's other side, and he was asking questions about her parents' trip. Anna offered to trade her peach half for Kobi's oatmeal cookie. "Okay," Kobi said, even though she really liked oatmeal cookies.

"Was it hard to wash away the famous artist's work last night?" Anna asked between bites.

"Yes. But I had to."

Lily, on the other side of Anna, was listening. Everybody around them was. Kobi liked the way the kids were looking at her today.

"Her parents are the subject of a *National Geographic* special," Norman announced.

Montpellier, Montpellier, Montpellier. If only the word that worked in cavernous places would get her out of this awful situation.

"And although I never watch TV," Norman said, "you can bet I'm going to watch *that* program."

Anna looked amazed. *"When? Why?"*

Now the kids at the table were really interested.

"When?" Norman said to Kobi. Before she could answer, he said, *"Why* is because her parents are on a sailing voyage to the South Seas and they're making their own tools for hunting and fishing and live in a tree house . . ."

A girl across the table said, "Norman, is this another one of your stories?"

"No," he said, his face turning almost as red as his hair. "It's the scout's honor truth. Tell them, Kobi."

She couldn't humiliate Norman now by revealing that he'd fallen for a whopper.

"*National Geographic* is making a special about my parents' trip when they return," she said dully.

"When are they getting back?" somebody asked.

"Soon," Kobi said, hoping with all her heart that this was true. When her parents got home, they'd take her away from Horace Mann Elementary, and she'd be gone before the lies caught up with her.

"Are your parents anthropologists?" one of the lunchroom ladies who had been listening asked.

Kobi didn't think so. And she didn't want to tell any more lies. "My dad is an amateur magician. My mother is a writer."

"Are *they* famous, too?" Lily asked, her tone sour. "Should we Google them?"

Anna shot Lily a look.

"They're not famous," Kobi said. She was going to walk the straight line of truth from now on, no1 matter what.

"Does your dad let you help him with his tricks?" someone asked.

"No. But he lets my mother."

"Does she wear a fancy evening gown and let your dad saw her in half?" Anna asked. "Is she beautiful?"

"She's very beautiful. She has long, wavy hair. But my dad doesn't saw her in half. He says that trick is too advanced."

"Do you know any magic?" someone asked.

"Our dad keeps all his magic secret," she said. "It's more fun that way."

"Let's go play Around the World, since it's raining,"

Anna said, standing up and looking at Lily and Kobi. Norman stood up, too. "Just girls," Anna said.

Norman sat back down.

"Has he ever told you why he wears striped shirts all the time?" Anna asked Kobi on the way to the classroom.

Of course he had. The first day.

"So he *blends in,*" Lily said with a laugh before Kobi could answer. "He has goats, you know. And in second grade for show-and-tell his dad brought a goat to school in a truck, and we had to line up and go outside and see it." She smiled and began to sing, "Norman had a little goat, little goat, little goat . . ."

Anna joined in. "I'd forgotten that," she said when they were done, and she smiled at Kobi.

Although she didn't want to, Kobi smiled back. The smile felt worse than the lies.

PHYLLO BUNDLE

FOURTEEN

$\mathscr{G}$RANDMAMMA called on Saturday. It was four o'clock in Paris and she had awakened from a nap feeling she simply had to talk to her babies.

Kobi explained that Brook had slept at Isabel's last night and wasn't home yet. Kobi hated the thought of Brook and Isabel, in their pj's, having breakfast together.

"It's nice that you girls are making friends," Grandmamma said.

Kobi didn't want Grandmamma to know she was so jealous of Isabel it gave her a stomachache. She didn't want Grandmamma to know that her only friend was an odd boy who had no other friends, and whom she was thinking of dumping because Anna and Lily made fun of him.

"Are things going well after school at the Hancocks'?" Grandmamma asked.

"Yes."

Kobi was glad Grandmamma seemed to be getting over her irritation that Uncle Wim had chosen the Hancocks for after-school care.

She told Grandmamma about the garden with bean teepees and rows and rows of colorful zinnias. "It's like an enormous painting," she said.

"Do you like Patricia?" Grandmamma asked.

It would make Grandmamma happy to hear that Kobi didn't, but Kobi said, "She does beautiful art."

After a pause, Grandmamma said, "Old habits."

Grandmamma wouldn't be jealous of Ms. Hancock if she knew about the Alzheimer's, but Kobi was sworn to secrecy.

"Grandmamma, are you famous?"

Grandmamma laughed. "Did somebody tell you I was famous?"

"No. I just wondered."

"Famous isn't necessarily a good thing to be, Kobi. The best things are to be good. And happy. And healthy."

Kobi hadn't been very good lately. And she couldn't be truly happy until her parents got home.

"That's what I want for Wim and for you girls," Grandmamma said with a catch in her voice. "That you be good. And happy. And healthy. That's enough for anybody."

It sounded like Grandmamma was crying. But why would she be?

"When are you and Mr. Gyver leaving on your trip?" Kobi asked.

"As soon as I feel a little better."

After she got off the phone, Kobi helped Uncle Wim fold laundry in the basement. He wasn't as careful as Madame Louise, and some days Kobi wore wrinkled clothes.

"Things going okay at school?" he asked, folding jeans that had been left in the dryer with towels too long and looked like a fuzzy animal had napped in them.

"I guess," Kobi said. She had thrown away the paper with Uncle Wim's conference time written on it.

"Anything coming up? Anything I should know about?"

"No," Kobi said.

"You've got a nice desk now," he said.

The desks and chairs had been delivered last night. Brook hadn't seen hers yet. They were identical—white, with curved metal legs, a middle drawer, and two drawers on one side.

"And since you've got that desk," Uncle Wim said, "maybe you'd like to spend a little more time on your school-work."

Kobi tried not to look away. Looking away was a sign of guilt. But Uncle Wim couldn't possibly know about the math. She changed the subject. "Maybe we could have a couch for the living room, too, if you can afford it."

"What's wrong with the black couch?"

"It smells like a rhinoceros," she said. "And it's scratchy. But if you don't have the money, it's okay. We won't be here long. And you pay Sally to keep us."

Uncle Wim looked surprised. "I'm not paying Sally to keep you. She likes you. And she thinks it's good for Patricia to be around children. I'm giving her money because her web design business has tanked since Patricia's Alzheimer's has progressed so much." He cleared his throat. "I can afford a new couch, Kobi. One that doesn't smell like a rhinoceros."

Kobi suspected from the way his eyebrows moved that he might not be telling her the truth. And her own guilty conscience made her mean. "Can you afford furniture for the dining room? Or the foyer? Or a table for the kitchen that doesn't wobble? The house echoes when we talk."

Uncle Wim gazed at her as if she were molting. Finally, he said, "Kobi, I can afford furniture."

So *temporarily* had worked! "Then why don't you have any?"

"Between you and me?"

Kobi nodded.

"I hope Sally will marry me soon. If she does, she'll want to decorate the house."

Kobi could imagine what Sally would do with the house. She would paint the dingy walls with brilliant colors like eggplant purple and morning glory blue. And she would fill the place with Ms. Hancock's artwork. She'd plant a beautiful garden in the scraggly backyard. And she'd be right here when Uncle Wim came home every night. *Razzmatazz* popped into Kobi's head as she thought about what an exciting, magical place it would become.

"Have you asked her to marry you?"

"I asked her to marry me years ago."

Kobi felt grown up talking to Uncle Wim about this. "What did she say?"

"*Maybe someday.* For half my life she has been saying that. That's why I bought the house. I thought she was on the verge of saying yes, and then—" He stopped. But Kobi saw the rest of the story in his eyebrows.

And then Grandmamma dumped her and Brook on him.

"So you're not unfortunate?"

An eyebrow went up. "Unfortunate? As in a poor unfortunate?" He ruffled her hair, which had grown half an inch since the stove disaster. "I used to be more unfortunate than I am now," he said.

She smiled to herself. *Phyllo bundle.* She felt toasty warm in the chilly, damp basement with Uncle Wim. The magic was working.

BUOY

FIFTEEN

ALMOST a week went by before Uncle Wim said on the way to school, "I'll be a little late getting to Sally's this evening. I have Kobi's school conference."

Kobi's eyes flew to his in the mirror. Then she looked away to stare out the window as if she had never before seen the Presbyterian church that they drove past twice a day. How had he found out?

"You're not supposed to go," she said. "It's for parents."

"Call me Dad," he said, winking at her in the mirror.

It was like a knife in her heart.

"Oh, Kobi. I was just messing with you. It was in bad taste," Uncle Wim said. "I'm sorry."

She tried to blink back the tears.

"Okay?" he asked.

She nodded, but she couldn't meet his eyes. *Why* didn't her parents get the boat seaworthy? If only the Great Alighieri would come home, everything would be fine.

✶

When Ms. Carlson had them get out their worksheets as usual, Kobi almost didn't bother with her fake one. She glanced up at Ms. Carlson as she passed. Ms. Carlson put her hand on Kobi's shoulder.

Kobi's heart stopped. Was she going to be marched out of the room in shame?

Ms. Carlson gave Kobi's shoulder a little squeeze and smiled at her, and then moved on to glance at Norman's worksheet. Today he was wearing a green-and-gold-striped shirt. He would blend in well with Sally's zinnias.

What did Ms. Carlson's smile mean? That she agreed with Kobi it was silly to worry about math when Kobi would be leaving at Christmas, if not before?

At lunch, Anna put her tray by Kobi's, which she had been doing all week. "Scoot over," she said.

Anna had plenty of room.

"Hurry," she insisted. "Scoot!"

When Norman arrived at his usual spot on Kobi's other side, there was no more space.

"This table is full," Anna said.

"No, it isn't," Norman said. "There's room. Move over, Kobi."

She tried to slide to the left, but Anna wouldn't budge and Kobi didn't try really hard.

"Come on, Kobi," Norman said again. "Scoot over."

"This table is full, Goat Boy," Anna said.

Norman's face turned fiery red. He looked at Kobi. When she looked away, he moved on to another table.

Kobi felt sick. She should get up and follow Norman. Anna had been terribly cruel.

After lunch, when they traded papers to grade each other's science quizzes, Kobi penciled a note, very small and pale, in the lower corner of Norman's paper. It said, *Would you like an autographed copy of one of my mother's novels?*

He was watching her write, but when she handed his perfect quiz back to him, he didn't look at her note. He acted like he blended in so well, he didn't exist. Or she didn't.

It wrenched her heart. He'd been nice to her the day she'd fallen on the playground. He was always nice.

"Please read it," she whispered. If he were Brook, she could say *pantaloons* and things would smooth out between them; forgiveness would come with a giggle. One of the words she'd never cracked the power of, *buoy*, came to mind. They'd been studying homonyms.

"*Buoy*," she whispered.

He acted as if he didn't hear, but eventually his eyes drifted to the corner of his quiz. When he looked up, his blue eyes shone. He grinned. He nodded.

Monday, she penciled upside down and backward on the corner of her notebook.

He nodded again.

Kobi could have floated out of her seat.

✱

When Uncle Wim got to Sally's that evening, he looked exhausted. His necktie was rolled up and stuck in his shirt pocket. He wasn't hungry, even though Sally had baked a squash from the garden and the smell of brown sugar and butter filled the kitchen.

Kobi wasn't hungry, either, though she was interested in the squash and had drawn a picture of it after Sally had cut it open to reveal the seeds. She hadn't cared a thing for the botanical drawings Mademoiselle had encouraged them to do, but Sally's fruits and vegetables and flowers fascinated her.

Uncle Wim's eyes landed on Kobi now and then and she looked away. She told herself it didn't matter. She'd be leaving Des Moines soon and math worksheets would be no more than a scary dream.

When they got to Uncle Wim's house, she went straight upstairs to get the footlocker key out of her keepsake box. Her mother's books were inside the footlocker. She didn't want to part with one, but Grandmamma had all of Beatrice Bonnard's (her mother's author name) novels in a bookcase in the foyer of her apartment for everyone to see. And she had extra copies in the storage room.

Kobi's keepsake box, where she kept pictures and little things, had been under her bed, but now it was on her desk. She went through the box carefully, pausing to look at the picture of herself and Mr. Gyver's prizewinning pig, taken at his farm outside Paris. She wished Grandmamma would feel better and they could have their honeymoon. She sorted through everything twice and then a third time, but she didn't find the key.

She barged into the bathroom, where Brook was getting into the tub.

"Hey!" Brook said, pulling a towel around herself.

Kobi rolled her eyes. She'd seen Brook's naked body twenty million times. "You don't know where my footlocker key is, do you?"

"Of course not. I wouldn't go anywhere near your precious key."

Kobi scowled. She couldn't remember seeing the key since . . . the Paris airport when she set off the alarm. She had carried the key in the pocket of the white eyelet dress. *Dimpling* had gotten it safely through security and back into her pocket.

She found the dress on the rod that Sally had installed for their hanging clothes in their closet. She felt inside the pockets. No key. She tried to remember. She had put the dress in the laundry and Uncle Wim had done the laundry. Maybe the key had fallen out of the pocket in the washer or dryer.

Although Uncle Wim was on his bed with folders spread

out and his laptop open, she asked him to go to the basement with her. He felt around in the washer and took everything out of the dryer and shook it. He pulled the washer and dryer away from the wall.

"Sorry, kiddo," he said. "What's in that footlocker, anyway?"

Not even Grandmamma or Brook knew.

"Some things," she said.

"Why do you need to get in it tonight?"

"I just do," she said.

"You're a fount of information." He touched her head. "What do you think Ms. Carlson said about you during our conference?"

The bare bulb glared, making the basement laundry room look scary, like a good place for torture.

But she wanted to find the key right now. School wasn't that important.

"Maybe the key got folded up with the laundry. I need to check everything," she said, turning toward the stairs.

"Hey, kiddo. Slow down. We'll find the key or pick the lock."

She didn't want anybody else touching the footlocker.

"I'll find it," she said, running up the stairs. "Don't worry."

In their walk-in closet, she shook out all her clothes, her hands trembling. The footlocker was more than a thing she needed to open to get a book for Norman. It held her parents' things. Special things they would need when they got home. If she lost the key it would be a sign of something she couldn't think about.

She threw a whole load of magic at it—*dimpling, honeysuckle, trillium, veronica*—and wasn't surprised that she couldn't think of where the key might be. Someone else had to want the key.

Brook. If Brook wanted to see what was in the footlocker . . .

"Brook!" she said, bursting into the bathroom again.

Brook was in the tub. She glared at Kobi.

"I'm sorry," Kobi said, covering her eyes. "Do you want to see what's in the footlocker?"

Brook was silent. "Why are you tormenting me?" she finally said.

"I'm not. Really. You want to see?"

"Well, yeah," Brook said, finally. "Of course."

Kobi let out her breath. "Okay." Now she could use her magic to find the key. *Trillium. Veronica.* She let out the flower words in a rush. "I have to find the key first, and then I'll show you."

"I know where the key might be. Remember the first night? When you said to throw our dresses over the oryx? The key fell out of your pocket and slid under the tub. I forgot."

Kobi let out an explosion of air and kissed her sister's wet face. Then she lay down and pressed her cheek to the floor. In the shadows, she saw what she was looking for. The key was cobwebby and dusty. She polished it with her fingers. She kissed it, too.

"Oh, spare me," Brook said. But she got out of the tub, dried herself off, pulled on her pajamas, and, her eyes shining with curiosity, said, "Show me."

Kobi was so relieved to have the key that she'd forgotten why she wanted to open the footlocker. But when the top went back and she saw her mother's books, she remembered.

Brook knelt beside her. "I've always wanted to know what's in here."

Kobi took out the five books with their mother's name on the spine and her picture on the back.

"Mom's books," Brook said, sitting cross-legged and holding each one, running her hands over them.

Kobi sniffed the next thing before handing it to her sister.

"Mom's shampoo," Brook said, her voice catching. "Orange blossom."

The next thing rattled when Kobi picked it up.

"Ramen noodles?" Brook said, reading the package.

"Mom made me ramen noodles every day when I came home from kindergarten at noon."

"Really? She never made ramen noodles for me."

Kobi shrugged. "You were eating at school."

She lifted out her dad's huge, heavy, satin-lined magician's cape with its secret pockets.

"I wondered what happened to this," Brook said, hugging it. Her eyes glistened with tears.

"His hat, his wand," Kobi said, putting them on the floor. "There's a white rabbit in our classroom. It's Dante."

Brook looked skeptical.

"And remember this?" Kobi asked, holding up another book.

"It's what Daddy was reading to us at bedtime," Brook said, taking Mr. Popper's Penguins from Kobi. "Look. His bookmark is on page thirty-two." She touched the Post-it.

The girls sat in silence. Kobi felt their parents right there with them. Brook brushed tears off her face.

"I'm glad you kept all this, Kobi," Brook said finally, rising to her knees. "What else is in here? What's in the bag?"

Kobi pushed her hand back.

"Didn't wooden blocks used to be in that bag?" Brook asked. "Did you save our blocks? I want to see them."

"No. You can't see what's in the bag."

"Why not?"

"Because it's private." That was what Brook had been saying to her lately.

Brook looked miffed, but she didn't try to touch the bag again.

After a while, Brook took both of Kobi's hands as if they were playing ring-around-the-rosy. Kobi felt how big the world really was. How far away Paris was. And China. She wished Grandmamma and Mr. Gyver wouldn't go to China. They could honeymoon at Mr. Gyver's farm. And her parents were such a long way off, on their island.

Finally, Brook let go of Kobi's hands and stood up. "I need to have Uncle Wim initial my daily planner," she said.

"Okay," Kobi said.

She put everything in the footlocker except for the book she chose for Norman. She locked the footlocker and put the key in her keepsake box.

✳

Later, when Kobi was in bed and almost asleep, Brook said, "Are you sure you turned the faucet off all the way?"

"Pretty sure."

Brook padded down the hall and in a few seconds padded back.

Kobi had almost dozed off when Brook got up again. Kobi knew what was coming. Seeing what was in the footlocker had made Brook worry.

After Brook's fifth trip to the bathroom, Kobi dragged herself out of bed and went along.

As they passed Uncle Wim's bedroom, where he was reading, he said, "Everything okay? You girls need to get to sleep."

"We're okay," Kobi said. She wished Grandmamma were here. Grandmamma knew how to comfort Brook.

Kobi stood by the sink with her sister. The faucet wasn't dripping. She ran her finger around the tip. It didn't come away wet. "We'll stand right here and count five hundred chimpanzees," Kobi said. "If the faucet hasn't dripped by then, it's not going to drip."

"Are you *absolutely* sure?"

"Yes."

Brook hesitated. "Five hundred is a good number," she said. "It can be divided by two, four, five, and ten. Those add up to twenty-one, which can be divided by three and seven, and those add up to ten, which can be divided by five and two. And those are prime numbers." Brook smiled, looking less pale and stressed.

Kobi nodded, glad she hadn't accidentally picked a bad number. "You count," she said.

As Brook counted the chimps to five hundred, the oryx gazed at them with his light-up eyes. He had become a friendly beast. Kobi hoped Sally didn't put him in a garage sale after she married Uncle Wim. *Phyllo bundle.*

CARILLON

SIXTEEN

"*Y*OUR teacher is going to be talking to you about a special math program," Uncle Wim said on the way to school the next morning. "She says it will bring you up to speed."

Kobi felt Brook's eyes.

Kobi sighed. "Why? I'll be going home soon."

"They can't just babysit you, Kobi. They have to actually educate you."

"Are you going into *remedial* math?" Brook asked, horror in her voice.

"It's not remedial math," Uncle Wim said. "It's a tutorial program. Like you have tutors when you're with Mom. Your teacher says you're doing great overall. She says you're adjusting to the change. She tells me you introduced them to the work of the famous artist Patricia Hancock."

The look Uncle Wim gave her in the mirror was so full of affection that Kobi didn't know what to say. She smiled, hoping he knew she loved the way he didn't get upset about things. Well, there was the stove the first weekend. But not about the math.

As they drove past the little brick church, the bells burst forth.

✳

"Did you remember?" Norman asked the minute she got to her desk.

"Yes." When she handed him the book she said quietly, "Please don't tell anybody. I have just a few left." She glanced at Anna and Lily, who were feeding the bunny.

"I won't. I promise." He looked so proud it made Kobi hate herself for the way she'd acted.

When Norman saw her mother's autograph, he beamed. "Now I have seven author-autographed books, but this is my first adult novel. I'll read it when I'm an adult," he said.

Anna came to them. She ignored Norman. "Look what I did last night. I printed this picture off the Internet so it looks like a postcard." It was the melting castle with the Golden Gate Bridge in the background. "Is Patricia Hancock still visiting her daughter?"

Kobi nodded, although *visiting* wasn't exactly the right word. Norman walked away, cradling the book.

"Would you have her autograph this for me? Please?" Anna asked.

"She doesn't give autographs."

"Oh." Anna looked disappointed.

"Her daughter doesn't like people pestering her."

Anna took Kobi's arm. "You're so lucky. Imagine knowing a celebrity! Do you think I could meet her? Maybe not *meet* her exactly. Just look at her."

Kobi paled at the thought. But she pretended to be thinking.

"She doesn't see her public much. But maybe I could ask her about the autograph." She stressed the *maybe*. "Norman is my friend." It felt good to declare it, like she was telling even herself that she really did have a friend. "I want you to be nice to him if I get you an autograph."

"Oh," Lily said, taking a step back. "To Norman?"

Kobi nodded. "And I think he should be invited to Lily's birthday party."

Anna looked doubtful.

"He's nice," Kobi said. "He's kind and smart and interesting. He just has trouble blending in." She reached for the postcard.

Anna said, "I'll see what I can do." With steel in her voice, she said, "But I want the autograph." Her look said *Or else.*

Ms. Carlson took Kobi aside. She asked if Kobi's uncle had talked to her about the conference.

"Yes," Kobi said. "I'm sorry I cheated on my worksheets."

"I wouldn't call it cheating. You found a creative solution to your problem—though not the best one for the long run. Ms. Lake, who'll be coming to get you first thing every morning, will help you get up to speed. You'll be back with us in no time."

✳

After school, Kobi showed Sally the postcard Anna had made.

"Ah," Sally said, looking at it. "I remember that day. Nancy Phillips invited me to her twelfth birthday party and I didn't get there until all the other kids were leaving because Mom was mobbed by people wanting her autograph and then we got caught in traffic on the bridge."

"The girl who printed this would like your mother to autograph it," Kobi said.

"Oh, Kobi, I don't know . . ."

"The girl who's asking says if I can get your mother's autograph she'll be nice to someone who's nice to me."

"I'd forgotten what fifth-grade politics are like," Sally said after a while. "I'll see what I can do."

Malleable, Kobi said silently. It was the right thing to do for Norman, and that was what was important.

Armed with Ms. Lake's encouragement and explanation, Kobi sat down with Brook at the table and got out her math worksheet. Sally went upstairs with her mother.

When they came down, Sally gave Kobi the postcard. On

the back, in black ink, was scrawled *Best, P Hancock.*

"Thank you!" Kobi told Ms. Hancock, but Ms. Hancock was going out the door. In no time, she had taken several chairs from the shed and was dragging them into a formation.

"Does she need help?" Kobi asked Sally.

"I don't think so. Looking at the picture your friend printed . . ." Sally shook her head.

As she followed Sally outside, Kobi thought about saying Anna wasn't her friend.

The neighbor who trimmed trees came out on his porch and asked Sally if her mother needed help.

"Maybe."

Soon his truck was idling in the drive. The truck had a folding arm with a bucket on the end.

"Thanks," Sally called.

The neighbor gave a salute.

Uncle Wim also arrived about that time, and Brook came outside to see what was going on. Ms. Hancock stood in the late-afternoon sunshine gazing into space. She wore a long orange scarf that ruffled in the breeze.

Kobi felt uneasy.

Ms. Hancock came to them. "So glad you could be here," she said, shaking Kobi's and Brook's hands.

Uncle Wim kissed her cheek.

Ms. Hancock searched his face. "Do I know you?"

Sally made a sound it hurt Kobi to hear. Ms. Hancock always knew Uncle Wim.

"I'm Wim. We met in San Francisco a long time ago."

"Ah," Ms. Hancock said. "It's nice to see you again." Turning away, she began to build the installation.

Kobi saw Sally trying to hide her tears. Uncle Wim took her hand and pressed it to his cheek. Kobi was so glad Grandmamma wasn't dotty. She wanted to put her arms around both Sally and Uncle Wim. She wanted them to get married and make the big house beautiful so when she and Brook went home they'd be all settled with each other. Ms. Hancock could have Brook's and her bedroom. *Phyllo bundle.*

The neighbor got into the bucket on the end of the folding arm. The bucket hummed up and down as he placed the chairs according to Ms. Hancock's direction.

A man walking a dog stopped to watch. Sally took her hand from Uncle Wim and wiped her tears away. The carillon rang out, playing a beautiful song. Kobi had never realized that Sally and Ms. Hancock could hear it, too. Ms. Hancock stopped what she was doing for a moment, then went back to arranging the chairs.

As the installation grew, the breeze became stronger and the sky looked stormy. Uncle Wim went inside to get Sally a sweater.

Finally, Ms. Hancock pointed to the red chair with fancy legs. She signaled the chair's placement and, when it was balanced on the very top, let her arms fall at her sides.

The old installation had been cheerful and full of energy. But this one—maybe because the chairs were faded now and the day was growing cold—gave Kobi a sinking feeling, like those moments on the phone when Grandmamma said, "Well . . ." and Kobi knew their conversation was turning toward the end.

Kobi didn't understand how the installation could make her feel torn up. It was a pile of dusty chairs. But she was so full of emotion that she had to stand up and clap, even though she felt sad.

Sally looked surprised. But then everybody applauded. Ms. Hancock bowed, her orange scarf brushing the grass. Sally hugged Kobi's shoulders and kissed her temple. Kobi hadn't thought she wanted anybody but Brook or Grandmamma or Mr. Gyver to kiss her, but she decided she liked Sally's kiss.

Uncle Wim's phone quacked. He glanced at the display and stepped away. Kobi could tell he was talking to Grandmamma. It was late in Paris.

Uncle Wim moved farther away and kept his back to them. Kobi tried to shake off the feeling of the installation so she could have a cheerful visit with Grandmamma.

When Uncle Wim got off the phone, he said he needed to talk to them. His eyebrows were very still. An ice cube started to melt in Kobi's stomach.

"Is Grandmamma okay?" Brook asked. "And Mr. Gyver? Are they in China?"

"They're in Paris," Uncle Wim said. "And they're going to be staying there for now. Mom's tiredness turned out to be more than jet lag. She may be ill with a condition called myeloma."

Kobi didn't want Grandmamma to have myeloma, whatever it was. *Squelch, squelch, squelch!* She wanted with all her heart for Grandmamma to be just a little tired and not sick.

"What's myeloma?" Brook asked, looking pale.

"It means Mom's bone marrow isn't working right. They need to do some tests to be sure."

"But Grandmamma will feel better soon, won't she?" Kobi said.

"Her only symptom is that she's tired," Uncle Wim said. "And Leonard and the housekeeper are taking good care of her."

Kobi needed to feel Grandmamma's arms around her. She needed to go back to Paris. *Ragout.*

"We should take care of Grandmamma," Brook said. "I'm good at taking care of people."

Kobi nodded. "She needs us. We have to go." *Ragout.*

Uncle Wim put his hands on their shoulders. "Mom said you'd want to come home. But mainly she just rests and has tests. Actually, she's going into the hospital for a few days next week. So here is the best place for you girls."

"I want to be with Grandmamma," Kobi said, unable to hold back tears.

Ms. Hancock rushed over. "Don't cry, pretty Beatrice!"

Somehow, Grandmamma's illness felt like Ms. Hancock's fault. "Leave us alone!" Kobi said.

"Let's go inside, Mom," Sally said, taking Ms. Hancock's arm.

"Mom really does want you to stay here," Uncle Wim said. "She convinced me of that. I told her we could all come. But she wants you to stay in school, and she wants me to take care of you."

Kobi sighed. Grandmamma expected people to do what she wanted. She got cross if they didn't.

"Grandmamma and Mr. Gyver will come for us at Christmas, won't they?" Brook asked.

"Almost certainly."

"Why almost?" Brook asked.

"Nothing in this life is absolute," he said.

"Some things are," Brook insisted. "They have to be."

As they left the Hancocks', Kobi turned her face so she didn't see the chairs. Everybody was silent in the car.

At Uncle Wim's, Kobi went upstairs and shut the bathroom door. She sat on the floor by the window and watched Uncle Wim rake leaves in the growing dusk. His pile kept blowing away. A squirrel ran across the roof and Uncle Wim's rake scraped the sidewalk.

If her parents would come back everything would be fine. Her dad would do magic tricks. Her mother would make ramen noodles and create wonderful characters and make them do anything she wished. Grandmamma would be well. Sally Hancock would marry Uncle Wim. Ms. Hancock would remember them all.

Why was it taking her parents so very, very long?

She had been horribly mean to Ms. Hancock. Kobi's heart ached to say she was sorry. But Ms. Hancock, all wrapped up in her illness, wouldn't understand.

When the bells tolled seven o'clock, Kobi wondered if Sally and Ms. Hancock were listening. *Carillon* was a pretty word. She'd tried to use it for magic many times, and nothing had come of it, but this time she felt a tremor. Her sorrow at what she'd done filled her heart. *Carillon.*

After a while, Kobi stood up, knowing it was okay. That what she'd done was forgiven.

In the hallway, she heard a terrible sound, like the squeak of a dry marker on a whiteboard, coming from their room. She ran. Brook stood rigidly, in an almost dark room, staring at socks on her bed.

"What's wrong?" Kobi cried. *Squelch.*

And then she saw.

Brook swayed back and forth. "Take it away," she said. "Hurry. Before something terrible happens."

Kobi picked up the sock that had no mate and put it behind her back. "Don't worry, I'll get rid of it."

"Forever? Absolutely?" Brook asked.

Kobi nodded. "Forever. Absolutely."

How would she make a sock go away forever absolutely? There were no magic words for such a thing. She had never wanted a word that made things disappear. She pulled on a sweater and went outside with the sock balled in her fist.

The toolshed door was open.

Inside, she found a trowel. In a nook of the yard on the north side of the house where ferns grew, and where Brook couldn't see from the windows, she began to dig.

"What are you doing?" Uncle Wim asked, coming up behind her and making her jump.

"Burying Brook's sock. Socks have to be in pairs. This one is a stray."

Uncle Wim leaned against his rake, watching.

"And I have to be able to tell Brook that the sock is gone for good," Kobi said. "That I am *absolutely sure*. So if you come across the mate, don't let her see it."

Kobi put the sock in the hole, scooped the dirt back in, and stomped the mound flat.

Uncle Wim took off his cap, smoothed his hair, and put his cap on again. "You're a good sister, Kobi Alighieri."

Uncle Wim was a good uncle, too.

SEVENTEEN

*O*N Monday, Kobi put the autographed postcard in a padded envelope that Uncle Wim gave her to keep the card from getting crumpled.

At school, Anna slid the card out of the envelope, saw Ms. Hancock's signature, and grabbed Kobi's hands and danced her around. "Thank you, thank you!" she said. She plucked Dante out of Lily's arms and put him in Kobi's.

Lily looked startled and then very angry.

"Oh" was all Kobi could say. She'd been longing to hold him for so long. She remembered exactly how he felt nestled against her. She gathered him to her face and kissed him between the ears. "Hello, sweet Dante," she whispered. If only the Great Alighieri were here.

She petted Dante, seeing the memory in his eyes. All this time. And such a long way from San Francisco to Des Moines. She wished he could tell her how he'd gotten here. It was a sign. A sign that everything was going to be all right. Soon Grandmamma would be well and her parents would return.

✱

The little square envelope was on her chair when she came in from afternoon recess the next day. She almost sat on it. A similar envelope was on Norman's chair.

Kobi opened the invitation. She didn't really want to go to Lily's party. She just wanted Anna and Lily to be nice to Norman.

Anna and Lily watched her from across the room. Kobi waggled the invitation and nodded. She mouthed, *Thank you.*

Anna looked pleased, but Lily's smile was icy.

Kobi pointed out the invitation to Norman before he could sit on it.

"What is it?" he said.

Kobi shrugged. "Open it."

He nudged it with his knee. "I think it's on the wrong chair. I don't get things like that."

"Like what?"

"Like invitations to parties," he said very quietly. "It's a mistake."

"No, it isn't," she said. "Look. I have one, too."

His eyes filled with embarrassment and she knew she'd made a mistake. "It's okay," she said. "You don't have to go. Say you're busy that day. Or say you'll go and then get sick at the last minute."

He picked up the invitation and put it in his desk. Then he sat down and opened his spiral notebook and began to write as if she weren't there. His shirt was striped brown and tan and he blended into the desks and chairs.

✶

A few days later, Anna came into the classroom without her pretty blond ponytail.

"What happened?" somebody cried.

Anna flipped her ponytail that wasn't there anymore. "I donated it. Ten inches whacked off. Mom took a picture of me holding it. It looked like an animal. And then I decided to get a Parisian cut like Kobi's."

Kobi thought Anna looked very pretty in the new style. But later, she heard Lily say to Anna, "I can't believe you didn't tell me you were going to do that! Why didn't you?"

"I was afraid I'd chicken out."

"Well, you look . . . *strange,*" Lily said. "I can't believe you're copying *her.*"

Anna's face turned red.

Kobi acted like she hadn't heard.

Anna and Lily behaved decently to Norman now, though

Kobi didn't trust Lily. At lunch each day, Norman sat on one side of Kobi, and Anna sat on the other. Lily sat on the other side of Anna. Lily looked as if she had a stomachache that was somehow Kobi and Norman's fault.

Anna invited Kobi home with her one afternoon after school. Kobi was nervous, especially since Lily was also invited. But Anna's mother was nice, and Anna's house reminded Kobi of Grandmamma's apartment. The rooms were big and full of comfortable, beautiful furniture. There were fresh flowers on a table in the foyer and pictures of people in silver frames.

Anna took Kobi and Lily to her room. Lily made herself at home. Kobi wasn't sure where to sit or what to do.

"So when will your parents be back from their trip?" Lily asked from her perch on one of the twin beds.

"Soon, I hope."

"Has a *National Geographic* crew been traveling with them?" Lily asked.

"Sometimes," she said after a pause.

She saw the look Lily threw Anna. Anna flopped down in a beanbag chair and kicked off her shoes. She motioned for Kobi to sit in the other one.

Kobi kicked off her shoes, too. The thick carpet between her toes felt nice.

Anna pushed her feet over until her toes, polished a sparkly purple, touched Kobi's. "We should paint your toenails," she said.

"Okay," Kobi said.

Anna leapt up to get the polish.

From her seat in the beanbag chair, Kobi thought Lily looked kind of silly sitting on the bed like an angry egg. And she had gum on her shoe. Kobi saw Anna looking at it when she came out of the bathroom with the nail polish.

"What?" Lily said, scowling.

Anna pointed.

Lily took off her shoe and looked. Her face turned red. She jerked a tissue from the box on the nightstand and began to scrub. The gum stretched into dirty pink strings and the tissue shredded and made balls.

Kobi watched, and Anna looked up now and then from her polishing. Lily glared at them as if the gum were their fault.

"Some afternoon I'll have to come home with *you*," Anna said.

Kobi caught her breath. She would die if Anna met Ms. Hancock. And she certainly didn't want Anna to see Uncle Wim's house.

"We'll have to do that sometime," she said.

"Soon," Anna said. "Your life sounds so interesting."

Lily went into the bathroom and flushed the mess of shredded tissues and gum down the toilet. When she came out, she sat on the edge of the bed. "What does your mother write?" she asked Kobi.

"Books."

"What kind of books?"

"For grown-ups."

"Why don't you bring them to school?"

Kobi didn't want to take any more of her mother's books to school. "I'd rather not."

"Why?"

"I only have a few, and they're special."

"But if I went to the library or a bookstore, I'd find them?"

"I guess," Kobi said.

"Or I could find them online, right?"

"I think."

One of Lily's eyebrows went up with a don't-you-*know*? expression.

"I'm pretty sure." Kobi felt her armpits get sweaty. She wished Lily would stop shooting questions at her. "She hasn't written any new ones for a while."

"What's her name?"

"Beatrice Alighieri."

"There," Anna said, standing up. "Don't your toes look nice."

★

"How was it?" Sally asked when she'd picked Kobi up and they were in the car on the way to the Hancocks'. "Did you have fun?"

Kobi took her first deep breath in a long time. She leaned her head back. "It was okay."

Instead of taking the usual way home, Sally got on the freeway and headed toward downtown.

"Where are we going?" Kobi asked.

"To look at a vacant lot. Eileen is with Mom and Brook."

Eileen was Sally's cousin visiting from Philadelphia for a few days. She was going home tomorrow.

"Why are we looking at a vacant lot?" Kobi asked.

"For a garden." Sally sounded so happy. "But Wim said not to get our hopes up."

"Why do you love gardening so much?" Kobi asked.

"When Wim and I started dating, there was a garden in San Francisco. Downtown, kind of like this." Sally waved at the warehouses and shabby apartment buildings in the neighborhood they were driving through. Downtown felt deserted in the evening. "Wim spent a lot of time at that garden. It seemed very foreign to me at first, but then I got hooked. I realized the aesthetics of the garden, and the complexity if you do it the right way. The balance. I think the garden became for me what Mom's installations are to her. So Wim and I have had this dream . . ."

They bumped over railroad tracks, and Kobi saw Uncle Wim's car parked under a streetlight. He stood waiting for them. Sally was out of the car almost before it stopped moving. Kobi hurried to catch up.

There was a FOR SALE sign that looked new. A small brick building with broken and boarded-up windows hunkered on one corner of the block. The rest was parts of foundations that stuck up two or three feet high in the weeds and the trash that was blowing around. Kobi turned up the collar of her jacket. Two homeless people pushed a cart along the sidewalk across the street. Uncle Wim and Sally were crazy. Who would want a garden here?

"What do you think?" Uncle Wim asked, grinning.

"The location is perfect," Sally said.

Uncle Wim nodded.

Perfect?

He put one arm around Sally and one arm around Kobi as they walked toward their cars. "It's getting cold. We can talk at home. But I wanted you to see it."

Sally hurried toward her car and Kobi followed.

When they were in the car, Kobi said, "I don't get it."

Sally laughed. "Sometimes I don't, either, Kobi. It probably seems crazy, but this is exactly the opportunity Wim and I have been waiting for. You don't know how many plots of land we've looked at the last couple of years. But none of them were as well located as this. Did you see the building down the hill with the lit-up parking lot and people kind of standing around? That's a homeless shelter," she said, without waiting for an answer.

Uncle Wim pulled away in his car, but Sally waited. "Use your imagination," she said, gesturing at the ratty, weedy patch of ground. "Imagine a block-long row of bean tee-pees. Imagine an apple tree on every corner. Imagine paths with flowers and a place in the middle for little kids to play.

Imagine chickens roaming through it all, eating bugs and laying eggs. Imagine people whose lives are hard, working as volunteer gardeners in the sun and breeze. Imagine the fresh, organic produce: potatoes, squash, tomatoes, peppers, beans, peas—all kinds of those things. We could grow *tons* of produce in a season. Imagine how glad people who can't afford healthy food would be to have it for free. Imagine how *beautiful* it would be!"

Sally finally stopped talking and looked at Kobi and laughed. Kobi had never seen her so happy. She wondered if Sally had always been that way before Ms. Hancock got sick. No wonder Uncle Wim had wanted to marry her for a long time.

Uncle Wim said he was less unfortunate, but Sally hadn't been able to keep her web design business going. Maybe because the block was so shabby, it didn't cost much. *Temporarily,* Kobi said silently. Maybe it was even free to someone who would use it for something so good.

✴

The next morning at school, Anna and Lily were waiting for her by Dante's cage. Neither of them was petting him, which was unusual. Lily had what Grandmamma called the-cat-who-ate-the-canary expression.

"Kobi, is your mother really a writer?" Anna asked.

"Yes."

Lily raised an eyebrow and held up the postcard of Ms. Hancock's melting castle with its autograph on the back. "Did Patricia Hancock really sign this?"

Kobi nodded.

"Are your parents really on a long, exciting sailing trip?"

Kobi wished they would stop throwing questions at her, but she nodded.

"Is *National Geographic* really making a program about them?" Lily demanded.

"No." Kobi had to get free of the lie. It was making her crazy. "I told Norman that because he said the sailing trip sounded so interesting they *should* make a special, and I said they were. It was a lie that popped out. I wish it hadn't."

"So you *do* lie," Lily said quietly, as if she'd never actually met a liar before—just heard about them, like sinkholes or Bigfoot.

"Haven't you ever lied?" Kobi said.

Anna's head swiveled to Lily.

"We're not talking about me," Lily said. She put her hands on her hips. "Isn't it true you're also lying about your mother being a writer?"

Ms. Carlson was watching them. Kobi saw her coming toward them. And suddenly, Norman was at her side. "What are you guys talking about?"

Lily's voice was loud. "Kobi said her mother has written books that are in libraries and bookstores."

Kobi felt everybody watching them.

"So?" Norman said.

"It's not true. And she admitted *National Geographic* isn't doing a special on her parents. I'll bet she's not even French. I'll bet she's from Idaho. Or Peoria."

"Her mother is a writer," Norman said.

"No, she isn't!" Lily was practically yelling. "I went to the bookstore and the library last night. They checked for me. No Beatrice Alighieri who writes books."

Norman gazed at her. "That's because she writes under the name Beatrice Bonnard."

Kobi watched Lily's mouth come open, then snap shut. "Oh, you're saying that to save her. Because she's your girlfriend!"

This morning Norman's shirt was black-and-white-striped, and Kobi watched in agony as his neck and face turned as red as an apple.

"Could we look it up, Ms. Carlson?" Norman asked.

Ms. Carlson was watching Kobi. "Is it okay with you, Kobi, if we look up the name Norman mentioned?"

Kobi nodded. She was *not* Norman's girlfriend. She felt her own face turning red.

"Do you want to give me the spelling, Norman?" Ms. Hancock asked. "If you know it."

"Oh, I know it," Norman said. "I have an autographed copy of one of her books and I'm going to read it when I'm grown up."

As he spelled for Ms. Carlson, a feeling of dread, like a fog, filled the room. Ms. Hancock's sad installation of faded chairs flashed through Kobi's mind, as did Grandmamma's voice and Brook's hysteria over the unmatched sock.

Kobi tried to remember all the magic words, because somehow she knew she was going to need them. *Phyllo bundle, razzmatazz, squelch* . . .

Beatrice Bonnard came right up. There was a picture of her mother. Kobi couldn't help but smile, and her hand went over her heart.

There were dates by her mother's name. 1973–2011.

"This can't be ri– " Ms. Carlson was saying, looking over her shoulder at Kobi.

"She's *dead*?" Lily cried.

"She's *not!*" Kobi said. "That's wrong."

Now even Norman was looking at her like she was a freak.

"She's on a sailing trip with my dad, the Great Alighieri!" Kobi looked around at the faces. "I hate you! *Hogwash!*" she spat at Lily. "*Hogwash!* You're stupid and jealous. I hate this school! I want to go home! *Hogwash!*" She was crying. She didn't want to cry. "I want Grandmamma," she sobbed. "Or somebody. Call my uncle."

✳

She waited in the nurse's room until Uncle Wim got there. The nurse asked questions Kobi didn't hear. Kobi was a stone. Uncle Wim would pick her up and put her on a piece of furniture at his house and she would sit there. Stones didn't have feelings. Stones didn't need anything.

Uncle Wim held her hand as they walked to the car.

They went to Sally's. It was raining, and Uncle Wim said hurry or they would get soaked, but Kobi didn't hurry. But she was terribly thirsty. So thirsty she could catch all the raindrops from the clouds in her mouth and swallow them.

Somehow Sally knew she would be thirsty and gave her a glass of water, which Kobi downed in one great, long series of gulps. Sally said she would go to Brook's school and get Brook because they should all be together.

While Sally was gone, Kobi sat by Uncle Wim on the couch. Ms. Hancock sat in a chair looking at them.

When Sally and Brook got back, Brook shrugged out of her raincoat and ran to Kobi. When Brook tried to take her hand, Kobi pulled it away.

"I have to hold it," Brook said, finding it and hanging on. "We're a pair. That's what the Great Alighieri told us."

Sally said they needed to eat—that people in shock needed food.

Kobi shook her head.

But Sally spread bean dip on nachos and sprinkled cheese and put them in the microwave, then held them in front of Kobi and Brook. Kobi's hands went straight to them. Her face and hands were wet from her tears. Sally handed her a warm washcloth, which made Kobi cry more.

Brook wrapped her arms around Kobi. "Do you remember the therapist Grandmamma took us to see when we first moved to Paris? Madame Alarie?"

Kobi remembered that Madame Alarie knitted clothes for her dog. She nodded.

"Madame Alarie told Grandmamma this would happen someday."

Kobi felt cold and tired, as if she weighed a million pounds. She curled up against Brook, and Sally spread a cover over them. It was a dark afternoon, and Sally turned on lamps. Kobi felt Brook's breath on her forehead, and Brook's knee dug into her side.

"Why did you keep thinking they were alive, Kobi? Grandmamma told us they'd drowned in the storm. We saw the urns with their ashes go into the ground." Brook sounded almost angry.

Kobi sat up, disentangling herself from the cover. That was crazy. "We did *not!*"

"Yes, we did," Brook said, her face wet with tears.

"I was there, kiddo," Uncle Wim said, moving their feet so he could sit down on the end of the couch. "We interred their ashes right before Thanksgiving. I came to be with you and Mom."

"That's why I said we'd seen Uncle Wim before," Brook said.

How could Kobi not remember something that had happened? Though lately she'd been having a strange, niggling feeling that Uncle Wim had been in her life before. "You're sure I was there?" she said to Uncle Wim.

"I'm sure. You were so little—only five. You didn't cry

or say a word. It was kind of like you were being operated by remote control. Your Alighieri grandparents were there, too."

Kobi could hardly believe what she was hearing. "Who else?"

Uncle Wim thought a minute. "A few other family members. It was private because . . ." He stopped and looked at Sally. "Because you girls were so young."

He pulled Kobi against his side. He was warm.

Sally was making chamomile tea with chamomile Kobi had helped her dry. "Were you there, Sally?"

"No. But Wim told me about it. What troupers you girls were. He wondered if you understood what was happening."

"Mom explained to you girls what happened. Brook, you were brokenhearted and wouldn't let Mom out of your sight after that." He squeezed Kobi. "You acted like you'd lost your hearing."

She had cracked the magic of *Avanti!* and seen her parents on the island. She knew they were okay.

She looked around the room. Ms. Hancock must have gone upstairs to nap. Sally, Uncle Wim, and Brook were looking at her like she might break into pieces right in front of their eyes.

She needed something to hold on to. She reached for a magic word, then shoved the thought away. The magic words were trickery. Her mother had lied to her.

Sally brought over four cups of tea and squeezed in between Kobi and Brook.

"Tell me everything," Kobi finally said.

"Well," Uncle Wim said, "do you remember that your dad was gone on a lot of trips because he was an oceanographer?"

"I mainly remember his doing magic."

"That too," Uncle Wim said. "But this was a work trip on a large research vessel."

"I thought it was a sailboat for the two of them." That was what she saw bobbing in the surf with a hole in the side.

"No, it was a big ship with several scientists and students on board. Bea wanted to go along to do research for a book, so she got a job as crew. They flew from San Francisco to New Zealand to get aboard the boat."

"We didn't stand on the pier and wave goodbye as they sailed out of the bay?"

"No," Uncle Wim said.

Then how could she remember that her mother was wearing a blue shirt as she waved at Kobi—the same shirt she kept wearing on the island, the shirt that got more and more faded? Kobi couldn't believe they weren't on the island. How could they not be? She *saw* them.

Sally handed her tissues and Kobi wiped her face.

"They sailed on September twenty-eighth," Uncle Wim said. "They planned to be gone for about two months. But in the middle of October, they ran into bad weather. The weather is supposed to be calm in that part of the ocean during the fall. This was an unprecedented storm. Their communications went out and they collided with another ship. Your parents and three others were lost at sea."

Grandmamma had said that. They were *lost at sea*. Lost things could be found. The flower words were good for finding lost things. Kobi pressed her hands to her ears, to keep the magic words away.

"Do you want me to stop?" Uncle Wim said.

Kobi shook her head and put her hands in her lap.

"The accident happened on October fifteenth, but Mom wasn't notified for a couple of days. The chance of survival wasn't good, but it wasn't hopeless, either, so Mom didn't tell you girls what was going on. But about a week later, bodies were found."

Kobi cried silently, letting her tears wet Uncle Wim's shirt. Sally rubbed Kobi's knee.

"About a week after that, DNA showed that two of the recovered bodies were Bea and Al's."

Sally stopped rubbing Kobi's knee, but she left her hand there. It kept Kobi from floating away.

"Is there more?" she asked.

"I was in grad school at Drake, but I went out to be with Mom when she told you girls, and I stayed a couple of weeks. It took that long to get through the red tape and get their bodies home. Their bodies were cremated and we had the memorial service right before Thanksgiving."

Kobi shut her eyes. She was a stone.

✳

That night, she woke up. Using the pool of streetlight spilling across her desk, she found the key in her keepsake box.

In the closet, she unlocked the footlocker and lifted the lid. Her hand found the soft sack of words. When she loosened the drawstring and shook the bag, the bits of paper tumbled out.

"What are you doing?" Brook whispered from the doorway.

"Nothing," Kobi whispered back.

Brook sat down by her. One of her knees touched Kobi's. "I woke up," she said.

"So did I," Kobi said.

"Do you want to turn on a light?"

"No."

"What are these bits of paper?" Brook asked, feeling around on the floor.

"Magic words," Kobi said. "Mama gave them to me when you were at school. Certain words were good for making the rain stop or finding things. Others worked well in airports and cathedrals. The cafeteria at school. Others made me feel good."

"Did Mama tell you that?"

"No. She just said the words were serious magic. I had to

figure out how to use them. Some of them I never did. The best one was the one that let me visit them on the island where they were shipwrecked. I could walk around with them, hear their conversations. I could smell Mama's hair. I could see how close Daddy was to having the boat fixed. All I had to do was say *Avanti!*"

She expected Book to say that was crazy. But Brook said, "A psychologist told Grandmamma not to rush you. He said we should show by the way we acted that they were never coming back, but that we shouldn't try to force you to accept it. He said someday you'd be ready. I dreaded this day so much, Kobi."

The furnace came on with a belch of air that stirred the slips of paper. Kobi began to gather them up and put them in the bag.

"How many magic words did Mama give you?" Brook asked, helping.

"Twenty-seven."

Brook was silent.

"Is that a bad number?" Kobi asked.

"It's a wonderful number. Twenty-seven can be divided by nine and three, and nine can be divided by three three times. It's like the snake eating its tail."

"And that's good?" Kobi asked.

"That's very good. Especially with threes."

They kept patting the floor for pieces of paper until Kobi thought they had them all.

Brook said, "You know why I have to do that thing with numbers? Why I have to line things up perfectly? Why I need symmetry? Why I have to keep checking and rechecking things?"

"To keep bad things from happening. Things you worry about."

"And do you know what I worried about most?"

"Grandmamma?"

Kobi waited, but Brook didn't say anything. Finally, she realized Brook was crying. Kobi touched her sister's leg. "Tell me."

Brook took a deep breath and said in a shaking voice, "Your understanding someday that Mama and Daddy are dead. Because it's so hard." Brook started to sob, and Kobi pulled her into a hug.

"Well, I know now." She hardly recognized her own voice. It sounded old.

The carillon pealed out four o'clock.

"I'm going to throw away the magic words," Kobi said. "They're fake." She felt suddenly, flamingly angry with her mother for playing such a trick.

Brook sniffed and wiped her face with her pajama sleeve. "Don't say that, Kobi. Have you read any of Mama's books?"

"No. Have you?"

"Isabel and I are reading one now. But you're not old enough."

Why did Brook think she was so grown up?

"The words Mama gave you let you create a world where you could escape and be happy. That's pretty magical." Brook yawned deeply. "Come back to bed. Get in with me."

"Go ahead. I'll be there in a minute."

Kobi sat in the darkness, aching with loneliness. Angry. Sad. Not really believing.

To Kobi,
from Norman

EIGHTEEN

$\mathcal{T}$HE days passed. Sometimes Uncle Wim brought her a homework folder from school. Both Ms. Carlson and Ms. Lake sent bright cards saying they missed her and looked forward to having her back when she was ready. One night, in the homework folder was a fat envelope with a Post-it that said *To Kobi, from Norman*. Kobi knew it was a story. She put it in her keepsake box. She would read it sometime.

Most days, she called Grandmamma. Grandmamma sounded both sad and warm, telling Kobi that now the worst part was over and she could truly start to heal. But mainly Grandmamma sounded tired. One Saturday, Kobi realized it was the day of Lily's party. And she felt bad because she'd insisted that Norman be invited. She hoped he had forgiven her.

One day, she called Grandmamma and begged to come back to Paris. Grandmamma cried and said she was sorry they were so far apart, but the best plan was for Kobi to stay a little longer with Uncle Wim, especially since Brook was settled in school.

"I could come by myself," Kobi said.

"No, my dear. You're too young to travel alone."

Kobi stared out the window at the chairs. They made her feel so sad. If she went back to Paris, even if Grandmamma would allow it, everybody here would be without her, and she would be without them.

Sally came in from raking leaves, her cheeks red. She yanked off her hat. "Did Mom go upstairs to lie down?" she asked Kobi.

Kobi caught her breath. She had no idea where Ms. Hancock had gone. She had been in her recliner only moments ago.

"Kobi?" Sally said sharply.

Kobi stared at Sally. She listened to Grandmamma's voice in her ear.

Sally ran upstairs and Kobi heard her call, "Mom!"

"What's all the commotion, sweetheart?" Grandmamma asked.

Kobi knew in her heart Ms. Hancock wasn't upstairs. "I have to go. We've lost Ms. Hancock."

"What do you mean you've lost her?"

"She's dotty, and I was supposed to be keeping her company while Sally raked leaves and now she's gone."

Sally was in the kitchen now, putting her hat back on. She glared at Kobi.

"Patricia is dotty?" Kobi heard the horror in Grandmamma's voice.

"I need to go," Kobi said. "Bye."

She hadn't watched Ms. Hancock properly and she'd told Grandmamma Ms. Hancock was dotty. She ran outside without her jacket. The wind made her teeth chatter.

"Mom's coats are all in the closet," Sally said. "She'll be freezing. You go that way around the block." She pointed. "I'll go the other way."

Kobi ran as fast as she could, calling Ms. Hancock's name.

When they met up, Sally was huddled in the shelter of a tree calling 911. Then she told Kobi to go back to the house and wait in case her mother came home. "All you had to do was *watch* her, Kobi," she said.

As Sally turned and walked away, tears scalded Kobi's cheeks.

Inside, she waited. She nearly leaped out of her shoes when the phone rang. It was Uncle Wim. She told him what had happened. "It was my fault," she said.

"Oh, Kobi. It wasn't."

"Sally said it was."

"Well," Uncle Wim said. "It wasn't."

Sally burst through the door then. "Who's on the phone?"

"Uncle Wim."

Sally huddled over the phone as if it could keep her warm. She turned her back on Kobi. Kobi went to stare out the window at the chairs. She didn't want to hear what Sally was saying.

When Sally got off the phone, she came to the window, too, and stood looking over Kobi's shoulder. Tears were running down Kobi's cheeks, but she couldn't wipe them with Sally standing there. She wished Sally would go away.

Sally put her hands on Kobi's shoulders and turned her around. Kobi couldn't meet her eyes. Sally wrapped her arms around Kobi and held her close, rocking from side to side.

"I'm sorry. Looking out for Mom is my responsibility, not yours. Of course it wasn't your fault she wandered off."

"Yes, it was," Kobi whispered into Sally's shoulder.

"No, it wasn't. It kills me, Kobi, that I'm not anybody's little girl anymore. That's all."

"I know," Kobi whispered.

✖

In the early afternoon, the police found Ms. Hancock and took her to the hospital because she was suffering from exposure. Sally called Isabel's mom and asked her if Brook could go there after school. Kobi and Sally spent the afternoon at the hospital watching Ms. Hancock sleep.

"People will think I'm a bad daughter," Sally said, staring out the window.

✦

When Uncle Wim arrived after work, Sally wouldn't leave to go with them to get food. So Uncle Wim and Kobi went to the lower level of the hospital and got a burger and fries and coffee for Sally and took them back to Ms. Hancock's room. Then they picked up Brook at Isabel's house and went home.

"It's looking like you have to go to school tomorrow," Uncle Wim said. "Think you can?"

Kobi shook her head.

Uncle Wim sighed. "I hate to put it this way, kiddo, but you pretty much have to. I'm scheduled to be in court and have no choice. Sally will be at the hospital with Patricia. And you probably don't want to spend the day there."

The hospital felt sad and smelled funny and it broke her heart to see Ms. Hancock lying there looking so frightened.

✦

The next morning, Kobi called Grandmamma on the way to school. It felt freeing to be able to talk to Grandmamma about Ms. Hancock's illness. She told Grandmamma about Ms. Hancock being in the hospital. Grandmamma listened and said she hoped with all her heart that Sally knew what a good daughter she was.

At school, Kobi's stomach turned several backward flips as she walked through the door. This morning she'd put on a beaded jacket Grandmamma had said would be perfect for a chilly autumn day. The jacket was too fancy for school, but Kobi didn't care. It was warm and beautiful.

Ms. Lake was standing outside the office and waved Kobi over. "How are you?" she asked, touching Kobi's arm.

"Okay."

"Your uncle texted me last night," Ms. Lake said. "He thought you might like to sit with me and catch up on stuff before you go to your room. What do you think?"

"Okay."

In Ms. Lake's office they sat at a worktable, and Kobi saw math worksheets. Ms. Lake had demystified math for her. She'd let Kobi see that even boring things had order and logic. If you added orange and blue to a canvas, you got brown. If you added numbers, you got sums, different sums for different numbers. Every time. You needed to know where you were going with word problems the way you needed to know where you were going with a painting. All this had been a great relief to Kobi. Ms. Lake had helped Kobi understand that classrooms worked in predictable ways, too, which Kobi hadn't been able to figure out because there were so many people doing so many different things at once. Kobi pulled the first worksheet toward her and took a pencil out of the cup. Being back in a desk chair with a pencil in her hand felt safe. She got up and sharpened the pencil. The whirr of the sharpener and the smell of the pencil anchored her. She sat down again, took a deep breath, and looked at the worksheet.

"Did you ever see something that wasn't real?" she asked, pretending to read the first problem.

Ms. Lake thought a minute. "I used to stay with my grandparents in Tucson for a week every July. One summer, there was an antique vase on the dresser that at night became a face staring at me. My brain said it was an antique vase, yet I knew it was a face. Some*one*. I wanted to tell my grandmother, but I was afraid to."

"What happened?" Kobi asked.

"I lived with the face for a week. The next summer, my grandmother had moved the vase into the dining room." She smiled at Kobi. "Why did you ask that question?"

"Can I tell you a secret?" Kobi asked.

"Yes."

Kobi told her about using *Avanti!* to see her parents, about the ways they took care of each other and missed her and Brook. "Am I dotty?" she asked.

"Dotty?"

Kobi circled her finger at the side of her head.

"No. You're definitely not dotty."

"Then why did I see them if they weren't real?"

"Because you were so sad you needed to comfort yourself."

"So it isn't my mother's fault for giving me the magic words?" Kobi explained to Ms. Lake the magic words and how they worked.

"You're a wonderful girl, Kobi. I'm sure your mother adored you and wouldn't do anything to hurt you." After a minute, Ms. Lake added, "She couldn't help dying. It wasn't her fault." She handed Kobi a tissue and Kobi wiped her face. "Can I tell you a secret?"

Kobi nodded.

"My older sister was killed in a car accident when she was seventeen. At night, in bed, when I was in that twilight place where I was almost asleep, but still awake, she came to me. She stayed for a while, made me feel better, and then I fell asleep. At first it happened on its own, but then I was able to make it happen. And it was a comfort."

"Do you still do it?"

"No. It was part of my grief. After a while—a long while—I felt better."

Before Kobi walked with Ms. Lake to her classroom, Ms. Lake told her they could swap secrets anytime. Kobi said, "Thank you."

✷

In the classroom, it was indoor recess because it had begun raining. Anna and Lily were feeding the bunny. Norman sat at his desk writing in a notebook. He was wearing a bright red shirt with no stripes. Kobi felt everybody looking at her even if they were pretending not to.

She went to her desk.

"Thank you for the story," she told Norman.

"You're welcome," he said.

"You're not wearing a striped shirt."

He shook his head.

"Why not?"

He shot a glance at Anna and Lily and lowered his voice almost to a whisper. "I went to the birthday party and my mom made me wear a dress shirt that wasn't striped. And," he said, lowering his voice even further, "I survived. I even saw television," he whispered, "and my brain is okay." His pale blue eyes were earnest. "I don't need to blend in so much anymore."

Kobi was glad he wasn't still upset about the invitation. She asked, "Does everybody think I'm a big fat liar?"

"I don't know. The counselor talked to us about how you needed to believe. About how you'd be sad now that you don't believe anymore. Are you sad?"

Kobi sat down in her chair. "Yes."

She missed Grandmamma and Mr. Gyver and Madame Louise. She worried Grandmamma wouldn't get well. She grieved for Ms. Hancock. She wished Uncle Wim and Sally would get married and take care of each other the way Grandmamma and Mr. Gyver did. She hoped they had enough money to buy the vacant lot downtown if it wasn't free. Most of all, she still wished with all her heart that her parents were coming home. It was very hard to believe they never would.

Lily came over with the bunny. "Would you like to hold Peter?" Lily asked. "He might cheer you up."

Lily didn't look snotty and mean anymore. She looked scared.

Kobi took Dante and held him close. He was so soft and sweet-smelling. His nose twitched. She lifted his paw and saw the heart-shaped freckle. "I knew it was you," she whispered, burying her face in his fur.

Kobi:
Pack dishes

NINETEEN

*O*N Thanksgiving, Sally and Uncle Wim got everybody involved in cooking. When the pumpkin pies came out of the oven in late morning, Ms. Hancock cut herself a piece and seemed to find it delicious.

"Let's all sit down and eat pie," Uncle Wim said, tugging Brook and Kobi away from the celery and nuts they were chopping for the stuffing. "Patricia has a good idea."

Kobi didn't think she liked pumpkin pie. It didn't look likable. But Ms. Hancock was watching and waiting for Kobi to take a bite. *Scrambled* popped into her head and she pushed it away. She cut a tiny tip off the pie wedge with her fork and put it on her tongue. She mashed it against the roof of her mouth. "Yum!" she told Ms. Hancock before taking a much bigger bite.

The next day, they began to paint the downstairs of Uncle Wim's house. Uncle Wim and Sally painted the living room and foyer a color Sally called Maybe-Calamitous Curry. Kobi, Brook, and Ms. Hancock were assigned the dining room.

Ms. Hancock had no idea who any of them were, but with a roller on the end of an extender pole, she turned the dining room ceiling a cheerful golden color called Marigold Moonrise. She hummed as she worked and sent tiny flecks of paint raining down on them. Kobi rolled paint on the walls, while Brook, with small brushes and a ruler, made a neat line where wall and woodwork met.

About a million times Ms. Hancock asked when and where the gallery opening was, and about a million times Kobi or Brook made up an answer.

The next day, they painted the kitchen what Sally called Calm Cream and hired a man with a scaffold to paint the stairwell, which Uncle Wim said was at least two hundred feet tall. They christened the color Perilous Peach. At the end of the day, Kobi felt exactly like she was living inside a bright garden flower.

That night, for the first time, they took Ms. Hancock to sleep in her room at West Harbor, where everybody was dotty. Sally had decorated the room with Ms. Hancock's art. When they got there, Ms. Hancock said the gallery was nice, but on the small side.

Sally cried on the way back to Uncle Wim's. Uncle Wim

asked her if she wanted to spend the night with them and she said no, she needed to be by herself.

On Sunday, they boxed up a few things from the Hancocks' house and moved them to Uncle Wim's. Brook and Kobi went up on two tall ladders and cleaned the chandelier in the dining room until the crystal teardrops sparkled in the sunlight.

Late in the afternoon, they picked up Ms. Hancock and, with the last of the winter sun lighting the dining room, they spread a sheet on the floor and had a pizza feast. Ms. Hancock called it *bohemian*.

When the sun dropped behind the trees, Brook turned on the chandelier. The way everybody went *oooh* made Kobi think of the Great Alighieri.

✳

The next morning on the way to school, Kobi told Grandmamma all about the house. "You'd love it," she said. "It's beautiful!"

The silence was so long that Kobi thought she'd lost the signal. Then Grandmamma said, "Do you still want to come home?"

If she said yes, Grandmamma would feel bad that she couldn't make it happen. If Kobi said no, Grandmamma's heart would be broken.

Kobi would give anything to be with Grandmamma and Mr. Gyver and Madame Louise. But Paris and tutors didn't feel like her life anymore. And deep in her heart, Kobi could hardly bear to say goodbye to the people here.

"I'd really like to see you," Kobi said. And soon she handed the phone to Brook.

✳

Later that morning, when Kobi was with Ms. Lake, fat snowflakes began to tumble down. By recess time, the snow was falling so fast they stayed inside. Kobi played Where in the World with Anna and Lily and another girl.

"What's that yellow stuff around your fingernails?" Lily asked as Kobi passed out the pieces.

"Marigold Moonrise paint." And she told them what she'd done over Thanksgiving vacation.

Lily said, "Remember the day you came to school with the painted arm?"

Kobi nodded. That seemed like a long time ago.

"Did the famous artist Patricia Hancock really paint it?"

Kobi felt her face turning red as they looked at her. "Yes."

"Is she really your grandmother's friend in Paris?"

"She was my grandmother's friend a long time ago. Now she's my uncle's girlfriend's mother."

"Does your grandmother really live in Paris?" Anna asked. Kobi nodded.

"And did you really live there after . . ."

Kobi nodded again.

"Pinky swear all this is true?" Lily asked, her expression saying she really did want to be Kobi's friend.

Kobi offered her pinky and swore.

"I'm sorry I was mean to you," Lily said. "I didn't know . . ." She shook her head.

"Sometimes people do things they don't mean to do." Kobi thought of letting Ms. Hancock wander off and almost freeze to death, and of humiliating Norman by making Lily invite him to her party. "It's okay."

✳

That night when she and Brook were upstairs at their desks, Kobi asked if Brook wanted to go home at Christmas.

"I want to be with Grandmamma and Mr. Gyver," Brook said.

Kobi did, too. So that settled it.

"But I like school," Brook said. "Actually, I *love* school. If we didn't go back to Paris, I'd get to be a peer tutor and wear a special pin."

Kobi wished they could be in two places at once. She stared out the window at the holiday lights dancing through the trees. She shut her eyes and imagined she was in Paris. She felt Grandmamma's arms around her. She heard Mr. Gyver's rumbling voice. She smelled the coconut kisses and madeleines they made on Christmas Eve.

The pipes shrieked as Uncle Wim got into the shower. The house would seem empty to him if they went back to Paris, but he would have Sally.

Kobi felt sure Sally was going to marry Uncle Wim. She

understood now that it hadn't been her and Brook who had kept Sally from saying yes. It had been Ms. Hancock.

★

When they got to the Hancocks' after school the next day, Sally had a row of Post-its on the counter with packing jobs to be done. One said *Kobi: Pack dishes.* As Kobi wrapped glasses with Uncle Wim and put them in boxes, she asked if they could afford to all go to Paris at Christmas.

From across the room where she was taking a lampshade off a lamp, Sally gave Uncle Wim a look.

Kobi wished she hadn't asked. It cost a lot of money for Ms. Hancock to live at West Harbor, and Uncle Wim and Sally might need money for the vacant lot.

"All four of us?" Uncle Wim asked.

"If you could afford it."

"There's enough money, Kobi." He cleared his throat. "Actually, we could afford to travel back and forth several times a year if you decided you wanted to live here—though I am not a good traveler."

Sally shut a cupboard door harder than necessary. "The Mallory family is super rich, girls. In the Bay Area you can't swing a dead cat without hitting something big and classy with the Mallory name on it. The family gives away enough money each year to feed a midsized country a caviar-and-champagne diet."

"Sally," Uncle Wim said, scowling.

Brook looked as astonished as Kobi felt. Kobi said, "You don't *act* rich."

"He never has," Sally said. "Not even when he was a kid. When Wim was growing up he refused to wear anything that didn't come from Goodwill." She smiled. "And that's still pretty much the case."

"*Why?*" Kobi asked.

"Because the garment industry exploits Third World people," he said. He looked at their puzzled faces. "If somebody else has already bought the clothes, I don't add to the problem by wearing them." He grinned. "Come shopping with me at Goodwill sometime."

Brook shook her head so hard her hair flew from side to side.

Kobi thought it might be a way to fancy down her Paris wardrobe and look more like everybody else. "Okay," she said.

"So do you even need to be a social worker?" Brook asked.

"Yes, I do," Uncle Wim said.

"Only because he loves it," Sally said.

Uncle Wim cleared his throat again. "And while we're on the subject of all this money stuff, girls, you should know your parents' estate is in trust for you. So it's very important you learn to manage money ethically."

Kobi wasn't sure what *manage money ethically* meant. But she remembered Grandmamma saying the world would be a better place if more people were like Uncle Wim. And that was probably what *manage money ethically* meant.

"I'm serious," Uncle Wim said. "You'll be in trouble with me if you *ever* discuss this with anyone else except Mom or Sally." His eyebrows said he was serious. "Understood?"

They nodded.

"Does this have anything to do with Grandmamma being famous?" Kobi asked.

Sally laughed. "Famous for marrying *very* well."

TWENTY

SINCE Sally needed the little room that had been Kobi and Brook's closet for her home office, Kobi and Brook had to move their stuff. Uncle Wim said that if they came back from Paris with him and Sally, he would buy them enough dressers and wardrobes for their clothes *and* invite them to the wedding, which was how Kobi and Brook heard officially that Sally had finally said yes.

"Does Grandmamma know?" Kobi asked.

"She does," Uncle Wim said.

"What did she say?" Brook asked.

"What do you think?" he asked, winking at them. "She's happy."

When Sally came upstairs with a box, Kobi threw her

arms around her. Sally's coat was cold and damp from the snow, and her hair had a few melting flakes in it.

"Are you going to have bridesmaids?" Brook asked.

Sally laughed. "So Wim told you."

"I would make an excellent bridesmaid," Brook said.

"Well, Wim and I are keeping it simple, so you may have to wait until Kobi gets married to show your stuff."

"*Kobi*?" Brook said.

Kobi shook her head.

Sally laughed and gave Kobi's shoulders a quick hug, then went to get another box. Brook followed, talking about bridesmaids.

Uncle Wim carried Kobi's footlocker across the hall. "You never did tell me what's in here," he said.

It seemed like ages ago since he had asked her if she had something in her footlocker that needed to be fed and watered.

"Do you want to see?"

Uncle Wim sat in the window seat. "Yes."

Kobi lifted the lid. "These are the books our mother wrote." She stacked them on the window seat beside Uncle Wim. "Shampoo." She opened the cap and held the bottle for him to smell.

He sniffed. "Orange blossoms. Bea was a California girl."

She handed him the ramen noodles. "That's what I liked for lunch when I was little."

A huge clatter came from downstairs, and Sally called, "Wim! I could use a hand."

Uncle Wim touched Kobi's head. "Show me the rest later."

After he left, Kobi looked at the ramen noodles and thought about cooking them as a surprise for everybody. But she hadn't used the stove since she burned her hair, and anyway the noodles had expired four years ago.

Kobi gathered up the noodles and her mother's books and went downstairs. Everybody was picking up highlighters, paper clips, and folders from the floor.

"The bottom came out of the box," Sally explained. "What's in your box?"

"Our mother's books."

She arranged them on the bookshelf that Sally had moved from the Hancocks'.

"They look nice there," Sally said. "People will see them first thing."

In the kitchen, Kobi put the noodles in the trash. Gently.

Back upstairs, she spread out her dad's cape, top hat, and wand on her bed.

"What are you doing?" Brook asked, coming in.

"Do you think we should give Daddy's stuff to Uncle Wim?"

"But he's not a magician," Brook said, going back across the hall to help unpack.

Uncle Wim didn't do tricks like the Great Alighieri, but he did make Kobi feel safe and loved.

Kobi settled the top hat on her head. It fell down over

her ears. When she took it off, she noticed a folded piece of paper tucked into the inner band. She unfolded the paper. It was a Post-it with a childish drawing of two bunnies. Her name, printed with the *B* backward, was on the bottom. She must have been about four when she did that. Somehow she felt like it was a sign from her dad that Uncle Wim was deserving of the cape and top hat and wand.

"Aren't you going to help?" Brook said, sticking her head in the door.

✳

That night when Kobi took her bath, she used her mother's orange shampoo. She and Brook could use it every day while it lasted.

She found Brook in the bedroom, on her bed, staring at the jumble on the floor.

"Tell me I can live with a lack of organization," Brook said. "Tell me bad things won't happen because there are five suitcases in your half of the room and only three in mine."

"Bad things may happen," Kobi said. She knew that now. "They will happen whether or not you have everything perfectly organized."

Brook lay back and shut her eyes. "I'm going to try deep breathing. Isabel does deep breathing when she's stressed." She opened her eyes and looked at Kobi. "What do you think about seeing the therapist Uncle Wim knows after we get home from the holidays?"

Kobi nodded. She had some things she needed to talk

about, and Ms. Lake was sometimes too busy to help her with her "math."

She took *Mr. Popper's Penguins* out of the footlocker. She removed the dog-eared Post-it that marked the Great Alighieri's place. She kissed it. She knew in her heart it was a goodbye kiss. Her dad would not touch the Post-it ever again. She closed the book and put it on her desk. She put the Post-it in her keepsake box.

Except for the drawstring bag, the footlocker was empty. She opened the bag and drew out a word. *Parsimonious.* She didn't know what it meant, and she'd never figured out how its magic worked. So why didn't she throw it away?

She held it to her nose. After all this time, she could smell her mother's touch on the paper. Or thought she could. She dropped the word back into the bag, closed it, and laid it on her desk.

She didn't need the footlocker anymore.

TWENTY-ONE

$\mathcal{T}$HE day before they were to leave for Paris, Norman called and asked if he could bring something over.

"What is it?" She hoped it wasn't a Christmas present because she hadn't gotten him one.

"Something you should have. In case you don't come back."

Kobi was planning to come back. She wanted to be here when Uncle Wim and Sally got married. She wanted to get up every morning and see Sally's face. She wanted to eat Uncle Wim's scrambled pancakes. She even wanted to go to a real American school. But once she got to Paris and wrapped her arms around Grandmamma, she didn't know if she could let go.

★

When she opened the door an hour and a half later, there was Norman with his cheeks flushed from the cold and his blue eyes gleaming. He pulled off his stocking cap, sending sparkles of snow into the air.

Kobi didn't see a car. "How did you get here?"

"Walked." He showed her a shiny new cell phone. "I found you with my GPS."

Uncle Wim was passing through from the basement with a load of laundry. "You walked all the way?"

Norman nodded, grinning. "Great GPS!"

"Well, stay until you thaw out, and then I'll drive you home."

"Wow," Norman said, looking around. "This is a bright place."

Kobi realized that Marigold Moonrise was the color of Norman's hair, which was sticking up as if he'd kissed an electrical socket.

"Kobi, offer Norman cookies," Uncle Wim called down the stairwell.

"Would you like cookies?"

"Sure," Norman said, working off his boots.

On the way through the dining room he stopped in front of one of Ms. Hancock's paintings. "This makes me think of your painted arm." He looked at the signature. "It should. Both were painted by the famous artist Patricia Hancock. Cool."

"She did all this," Kobi said, waving her arm. She told him about Uncle Wim and Sally getting married soon.

"So will Patricia Hancock live here?" he asked, awe in his voice.

"No," Kobi said, putting cookies on the table. "Can I tell you something private?"

"Yes."

"She just moved to a special place for dotty people."

"What are dotty people?"

Kobi circled her finger beside her head.

"Oh." Then he said, "My great-grandmother is that way."

Norman took something out of his shirt pocket. "Shut your eyes and hold out your hand, please."

"It's not alive, is it?"

"No."

When Kobi opened her eyes, she saw a beautiful metal and iridescent glass beetle about the size of a nickel. It reminded her of the one Norman had given her the second day at Horace Mann Elementary.

"You had to set the real one free," Norman said. "But this one you can keep to remember."

It was hard to read Norman's face. Maybe he was talking about more than beetles.

"Do you think kids are ever dotty?" Kobi asked.

"I don't know any who are," Norman said. "Why?"

She explained about the magic words. "I could *see* my parents. I could watch what they were doing. Sometimes my dad was fishing, sometimes he was making things they needed like nets and traps and a whole entire tree house that it took him forever to build. I could see my mom doing laundry in the surf and combing her hair. I could hear the waves and the rustling of the trees in the wind. I could smell the flowers. I could see them sleeping under the stars. I saw them every single day. A lot."

Norman gazed at her.

"Remember the day you said it was almost like I'd been there?"

He nodded.

"And now I know they weren't there," Kobi said, her voice catching. "But they were *real* to me." She swallowed. "So am I dotty?" Ms. Lake had said she wasn't, but teachers didn't know everything.

"I'm a kid, okay? Not like a doctor or something. But I think you just have a wonderful imagination. Think what you created, Kobi! Remember, you're the daughter of a famous writer."

Kobi felt herself smiling. "And a magician. Do you believe in magic?"

"I believe in real magic. What you just told me was pretty magical. Every time I write a story I feel like I've done serious magic."

After a while, she and Uncle Wim took Norman home.

"Goodbye," he said. "I hope you come back."

"Me too," she said.

✷

When she got home, she went into the room that was becoming Sally's office. In an open box, she saw Post-its. She wrote *I ♡ you* on two of them. One she stuck on Sally's purse, which was on the floor in the foyer in front of the bookshelf holding Beatrice Bonnard's books. One she stuck on the mirror over the sink in the little bathroom off the kitchen where Uncle Wim shaved every day.

IRIDESCENCE

TWENTY-TWO

*O*N the way across the ocean, Kobi held Uncle Wim's hand when the plane experienced turbulence. He was pale and clammy, as if he couldn't wait to get out of the cabin and safely on the ground. He grumbled about how Grandmamma had moved to Paris when she knew he couldn't stand to fly.

When they finally landed, Grandmamma and Mr. Gyver were waiting outside the security gates. Grandmamma was waving like a windmill and Mr. Gyver was beaming. Kobi and Brook bolted, leaving Uncle Wim and Sally behind.

Both Kobi and Brook managed to get their arms around her at once, and Grandmamma's happy tears fell first on one and then on the other. And then Mr. Gyver was hugging them, and he smelled like toothpaste and the little brown cigarettes he wasn't supposed to smoke.

Kobi's heart danced when Grandmamma opened her arms to Sally and said, "I'm so pleased for you and Wim, Sally."

Then Mr. Gyver kissed Sally on the cheek and said, "I'm sorry to hear Patricia is ill."

Sally flushed. "Thank you."

Uncle Wim, seeming to feel much better, hugged Grandmamma, rocking her from side to side. "You're looking good, Mom," he said. Then he shook hands with Mr. Gyver. And then he hugged him, too.

✴

At the apartment, which smelled so heavenly Kobi nearly floated off the floor, Madame Louise greeted them in French, which was what she did when she was emotional, calling them her precious little *mesdemoiselles* and pulling them down the hallway into the kitchen.

Everything was exactly as Kobi remembered it except a million times more wonderful. She was *home*. And there were the coconut kisses on a plate waiting for them. "But not the madeleines," Madame Louise said. "Tonight!"

Under the tree in the living room, when Kobi finally got there, were about a million presents. In the late-afternoon light, the tree twinkled with silver.

Kobi sat on the floor beside Grandmamma and leaned against Grandmamma's legs. Grandmamma stroked her hair. "You got a haircut," she said.

"Yes," Kobi said, skipping over her cooking adventure and to the amazing part. "I started a new fashion at my school." Maybe by spring break, which was the next time Kobi would be returning to Paris, even Lily would have short hair.

"How are you feeling?" Kobi asked, looking into Grandmamma's face. Grandmamma looked older, but very pretty.

Grandmamma shrugged. "I rest a lot. But life is good." She smiled at Mr. Gyver. "Leonard sees to that."

Mr. Gyver looked at Uncle Wim and Sally. "Do you two have a wedding date?"

"January tenth," Uncle Wim said.

"I'm going to be a bridesmaid," Brook said.

Sally laughed. "Of sorts." She explained how they'd be married in a judge's chambers, but Kobi and Brook would stand before the judge with them.

"I'm so happy for you," Grandmamma said. "It's a blessing to my babies." She touched Kobi's and Brook's heads. "And they will be blessings to you."

Even Uncle Wim got tears in his eyes. And then Madame Louise said dinner was ready and they all went into the dining room, where candles sparkled everywhere and Brook and Kobi snuck each other satisfied looks as they ate real food.

✴

After dinner, when they were buttering and flouring the madeleine tins, Kobi asked Madame Louise if Grandmamma felt well most of the time.

"She is her old self some days. Other days, the medicine makes her need lots of naps." Madame Louise shrugged. "You girls are the best medicine for her."

"We'll be back in March," Kobi said.

"And we'll be back again this summer," Brook said, "for a month."

"Good," Madame Louise said.

✱

After the madeleines were out of the oven and cooling, they opened the mountain of presents, which took a long time. On one side of Kobi, books, games, stuffed animals, pretty bracelets and necklaces, soft sweaters and robes and cozy slippers grew into a pile. On the other side, cast-off paper, satin ribbons, and torn boxes grew even higher. Kobi could read Uncle Wim's eyebrows saying *Too much, too much*. But Grandmamma put her hand on his knee. And when Grandmamma wasn't looking, Uncle Wim winked at Kobi.

When Grandmamma opened her gift from Kobi and saw the wide, colorful friendship bracelet Kobi had learned to make in art class, Grandmamma asked Kobi to tie it on her wrist. Kobi had knotted one for every single person in the room: Madame Louise, Grandmamma, Mr. Gyver, Uncle Wim, Sally, and Brook. Kobi had thought her fingers would fall off and she would go blind before she was done with them all. And although nobody knew, she had given the most perfect one to Ms. Hancock.

Everyone was quiet after the last of the presents were opened.

Madame Louise stood and asked Kobi and Brook if they'd like to help serve. Even with the clatter of plates, cups, glasses, and trays, the house seemed hushed.

When the madeleines and tea were on the low table in front of the fireplace, Mr. Gyver poured champagne for the grown-ups and sparkling cranberry juice for Brook and Kobi.

Looking around the room at all of them, he gave his usual toast, *"L'chaim!,"* which Kobi knew meant "to life."

★

At bedtime, while Brook was taking a bath, Kobi went to the kitchen for a coconut kiss and found Grandmamma making tea.

"I know it's bedtime," Grandmamma said, "but I'm too happy to sleep. How about you?"

Kobi nodded and gave Grandmamma a huge hug just because she could.

"Sally seems so good to you girls," Grandmamma said, sitting down at the table.

"She is." Kobi got a cookie and sat across from her. "Why didn't you like Sally?" Kobi asked. "Why did you always call her Sally Hancock?"

"Oh, sweetie, there's not a mother alive who thinks a girl is good enough for her son. It's the way of the world," Grandmamma said.

"But you said Sally wasn't Uncle Wim's girlfriend," Kobi reminded her.

Grandmamma sighed. "A mother can dream. And hide her head in the sand. The real truth is that Patricia and I have a history. She stole my boyfriend."

Kobi tried not to laugh. But it was hard to imagine Grandmamma and Ms. Hancock fighting over boys. "What happened?"

Grandmamma's face had a really-shouldn't-talk-about-it look.

"It can be a bedtime story," Kobi said. "Tell me."

"It will put us both to sleep, that's for sure."

As Grandmamma sipped her tea, she talked about living in a sorority house, about parties and boyfriends. She talked about meeting this special boy, Leonard Gyver, who rang her bells. And her dear friend, a sorority sister, luring him away.

"I could never forgive her," Grandmamma said. "But I acted like I did and was in their wedding party. And then Patricia refused to take Leonard's name—that precious name that I would have given anything for! I couldn't have it, and she didn't want it. The irony!" After all these years, Grandmamma still looked upset. She drew her robe around her. "And then there was all that fuss about her *art*. Everybody always talking . . . Patricia Hancock this and Patricia Hancock that." Grandmamma shook her head. "But I caught up with her after my first husband's death, dear man."

"What did you do?"

"Married well," Grandmamma said, beaming. "Mallory is a much bigger name than Hancock."

"So were you famous?" Kobi asked.

Grandmamma shrugged. "In my way, I guess. For a few years." She stifled a yawn. "I shouldn't have let you get me started on this old stuff. I'm blessed beyond measure that Sally loves you girls. I wish I could undo the way I treated Patricia and Sally."

It was kind of the way Lily had treated Kobi.

"You're treating Sally nicely now," Kobi said. "And Ms. Hancock doesn't care anymore."

Grandmamma rinsed her cup and put it in the sink. "I'm glad you're kind to Patricia. For my sake." She gave Kobi a kiss. "Sleep tight."

"You too."

★

But Kobi couldn't sleep. It was so quiet inside Grandmamma's thick-walled, deeply carpeted apartment. All she could hear was Brook's breathing and the clock on the dresser ticking. Kobi missed the barking of the dog across the street and the tolling of the bells in the carillon tower. She missed the sounds of Uncle Wim moving around. Although she was happy and cozy, she was eager to get back. She was eager for spring to come and the vacant lot that Uncle Wim had bought to become an amazing, beautiful garden that all kinds of people could enjoy.

She got up, stepped into her slippers, wrapped herself in a blanket, and stepped out onto the terrace. The stars were so brilliant, and the lights of Paris sprinkled the skyline with colors. The word *iridescence* came into her mind unbidden.

The floor of the balcony was the floor of the tree house. The *shush* of the light midnight Paris traffic was the sound of the sea when the tide was out. The blanket warming her was her parents' arms.

She opened her eyes. She could never go to the island again, but her parents were there, together, and they loved her and Brook. Her mother was not a liar and the Great Alighieri wasn't a trickster. Real magic was as real as the stars.

Magic Words

· · · · · · · · · · · · · · · · · · ·

Magic word, alphabetized	Use of magic word
Avanti!	Lets Kobi see her parents going about their lives on the island.
Buoy	Makes people understand you really are sorry.
Caribou	Lets a person know you love her and she can go away but that she must come back.
Carillon	Lets a person know she's been forgiven.
Dilettante	Protects people from finding out things they shouldn't know.
Dimpling	Safeguards tiny things like keys and beetles.
Fiddlesticks	Helps with dilemmas.
Freesia	Makes people want to purr.
Frippery	Does not make hair grow.
Hogwash	Sometimes takes care of mean people.
Honeysuckle	Helps find things.
Iridescence	Brings moments and memories alive in fine, glowing detail.
Lingua franca	unknown
Malleable	Helps people decide to do the right thing.

Mayfly	Stops rain.
Montpellier	Works to make good things of all kinds happen in large, cavernous places like cathedrals, museums, stadiums, gymnasiums, and airports.
Pantaloons	Lets Kobi and Brook make up with each other without a lot of discussion.
Parsimonious	unknown
Phyllo bundle	Makes things seem cozy.
Ragout	Makes life better for sick people.
Razzmatazz	Opens the door to exciting things.
Scrambled	Makes food that isn't real food taste yummy.
Snapdragon	An impatient, foot-stomping word that makes things happen right now!
Squelch	Calms things down.
Temporarily	Makes life better for unfortunate people.
Trillium	Helps find things.
Veronica	Helps find things.

Acknowledgments

....

Gratitude to friends and colleagues who nurtured this project: the Prairiewoods Retreat Group who heard the bare bones of the story in 2009; my writers' bloc (Jan Blazanin, Rebecca Janni and Eileen Boggess); Susan Cohen and her team at Writers' House; Mary Cash and her crew at Holiday House. And all the people whose names I don't know but whose dedicated work I see at every turn. Thanks!